Evelyn

and the

Kung Fu Headmaster

KWAN WU

Evelyn and the Kung Fu Headmaster

Author: Kwan Wu
Project Director: Chun Ng

Published by Kwan and Chun Publishing Ltd,
a company registered in England and Wales.

ISBN: 978-1-8380984-1-4 (paperback)
ISBN: 978-1-8380984-2-1 (eBook)

CONTENTS

CHAPTER 1

Born to Fight

The sun rose up as usual, shining on the unusual world of year 2130. On this cold November morning in London, rays of sunlight were dancing upon the shiny bodies of the robot workforce. Construction robots, which were made of steel, could be seen laying bricks at a building site. Sanitation robots, which had just finished their nightly clean, were welcoming the new day with rows of sterilised streets. Further out, the main roads were already busy with all sorts of self-driving cars.

Everything seemed peaceful, except that there were rumours in the air – rumours about a "shapeless evil" that could penetrate walls and kill …

At that moment, without anyone noticing, a self-driving car veered itself off the main road. Once on the side street, the car roared, and then went full speed towards a wall. There was a loud bang as the wall crumbled. The crash left a huge hole in the wall, exposing a gas pipe. The leaked gas triggered a series of explosions, which instantly turned the car into a red hot fireball.

All over the street, pedestrians screamed. Police robots dashed forward with fire extinguishers, but it was too late. By the time the fire was doused, the car was totally burnt down, and the unfortunate passengers trapped inside had already perished.

Meanwhile, in an airfield not far away, three computer scientists had just gathered. They had been invited to their chief scientist's mansion in the Scottish Highlands.

"You know, in all the years I've worked with Ronald, he's never invited us to celebrate his birthday," said Bradley, who was Ronald's deputy.

"That means it must be about something else!" Suzanne chimed in. She was the newest member to Ronald's team.

Bradley nodded, "Could be."

"Do you think it's about the shapeless evil which he's privately investigating these days?" Ethan asked, looking thoughtful.

"A major breakthrough perhaps?" Suzanne suggested, her eyes widening in wonder.

"Something like that … anyway, if Ronald needs any help, I'm going to say yes," said Ethan, who had always admired Ronald.

The engine started, and air swirled wildly around them. Noisily but steadily, their helicopter rose into the sky. The helicopter ran on autopilot, yet Bradley wouldn't keep his eyes off the flight data – he was a qualified pilot and still manually flew helicopters as a hobby. The others, however, were able to enjoy the stunning view of London from above.

They could see the historic London Bridge. On both sides of River Thames, there was an orderly flow of smart trains, smart cars and smart motorcycles – all coexisting in harmony under a smart road network.

The most eye-catching building in the horizon must be Stewart Tower. This was the headquarter of TT Stewart Corporation, a leading robot company in Europe which this team of computer scientists worked for. The iconic tower had a glamorously sleek and curvy design. It was also the tallest building in London, its pinnacle piercing into the clouds.

Ethan and Suzanne were staring out of the helicopter windows when Bradley suddenly shouted a warning: "Hold tight!" Next second, the helicopter started to nosedive.

Suzanne's face turned pale, and Ethan widened his eyes in shock. They were heading for the ground – faster and faster their helicopter was falling. Bags were dislodged and crashed towards the cockpit, breaking a side window. Glass shattered onto their clothes and wind began to howl into the cabin ominously.

"Hold tight!" Bradley repeated loudly as he shifted to manual pilot and tried to regain control of the helicopter.

Ethan and Suzanne could see smoke coming out of the main rotor. They were quiet as they braced for impact: any moment now, their helicopter could burst into flames and there would be no escape …

But that didn't happen, because Bradley somehow managed to bring their helicopter under control. They were, by some miracle, up in the sky once more.

"I can't believe it. We almost died!" Suzanne exclaimed, massaging her sprained ankles.

"Need any help? I've got bandages here," said Ethan.

Suzanne shook her head. She turned to Bradley. "What just happened? Was it mechanical failure, or maybe the shape –"

"It was the shapeless evil – a computer virus – attacking our helicopter's autopilot," Bradley replied, his brow furrowed.

"Why –" Suzanne began.

"Ask Ronald when you see him. He has observed this computer virus for a while now," said Bradley.

"How far are we from his mansion?" This was Suzanne's first time to Ronald's house.

"Look, it's just over there," Ethan told her, pointing to their right.

Fischer Mansion was shrouded in mist under the winter sky. Standing on the top of a cliff, it oversaw a foaming bay in the Scottish Highlands. As their helicopter descended into the picturesque landscape, they could see eagles soaring, waterfalls tumbling, and sheep grazing in the pastures around. The natural beauty around Fischer Mansion was a rare sight in this high-tech age.

Suzanne, who grew up in London, thought it was too rustic to her liking.

"That's Ronald's house?" she asked, cocking an eyebrow.

"Yes, it was handed down to him from his ecological architect great-grandfather," Ethan replied enthusiastically.

"No wonder," said Suzanne, sounding disappointed.

Ethan chuckled. "Appearances can be deceiving, wait till you get inside!"

Their helicopter touched down safely. Ronald ran out of his house to greet them. He was a tall, slim man in his forties, his loose-fitting shirt billowing in the strong and gusty wind of the Scottish Highlands. Trailing behind Ronald were their other team members, John and Florence.

"Welcome to Fischer Mansion!" Ronald called out, smiling broadly. Then he noticed the broken window, and his smile faded. "It's cold out here. Let's get inside my house." He led them up a cobblestone path.

Ronald's house was very spacious and high-tech. As they stepped in, they were amazed by the ceiling, which looked indistinguishable from the real sky. The ceiling turned out to be an adjustable electronic screen with options such as sunny day, cloudy night, thunderstorm and blizzard.

Ronald led them straight to the living room. There were smart sofas along the walls which could regulate their own temperature, and a smart tea table which could walk itself to other parts of the room. The cushions were simply awesome, offering massage, soft music and even perfume therapy. In the middle of the living room was a grand chandelier with hundreds of exquisitely-shaped prisms hanging from it. It looked very elegant and was probably worth a fortune.

Ronald's children came down the marble staircase to say "hello". They were a pair of adorable twin girls aged seven. Ronald kissed his children on the cheeks, then sent them back to their rooms because "Daddy needs to work". The girls were visibly displeased – one of them pouted, the other pulled a face – but both obeyed their father without arguing.

"So what happened on the helicopter?" Ronald asked impatiently.

"We nearly died!" said Suzanne in a dramatic tone.

"It was the computer virus you told me about," Bradley answered sensibly, "I saw its viral patterns in our helicopter's autopilot."

For a few seconds, there was silence in the room.

"I'm glad all three of you survived," Ronald said suddenly. "We know that the computer virus has a name now: it calls itself Victor –"

"Oh my god!" Suzanne gasped, horrified. "The shapeless evil calls itself Victor!"

Ronald nodded and continued, "Currently, Victor's lurking in various computer systems. I've observed the Victor virus causing accidents … at first, the accidents mainly occurred on the roads; but now, they are also happening at sea and in the air."

"What exactly is Victor seeking?" asked John seriously. "I mean, why is this computer virus killing people in the real world?"

"Look, why else would it call itself Victor?" said Ronald. "Clearly, it wants to be the 'victor' in this war against the human world!"

Suzanne shivered, but Ethan suddenly became very excited.

"Then how are we going to fight Victor?" the young scientist asked, jumping up.

"Fighting Victor's not part of your Stewart Corp duty, obviously," answered Ronald, looking thoughtful. "Therefore, the choice is yours: You may either take the opportunity to save the world with your computer expertise, or else you may forget what I said today."

Ronald then glanced at his team. He was met with eager faces, sparkling eyes and an anticipation that was almost tangible …

"All right," he said decisively, "there's something I need to show you!"

They followed Ronald out of his mansion to the edge of the cliff, where there was a very narrow path. They walked in the cold, howling wind, holding onto a swaying rope to steady themselves. Looking down the cliff, they could see a coast full of jagged rocks hundreds of metres below them.

"How far are we –" asked Suzanne, but Ronald had stopped walking.

"Welcome to my cave," he said mysteriously, pointing towards a hidden door next to him.

Ronald opened the wooden door – yellowish light instantly poured out of the cave. His team was shocked by what they saw … they didn't expect to see so many highly realistic humanoid robots in such a natural, inconspicuous cave! The robots were all standing like statues against the wall. The females had smooth, glowing skin and were very pretty; the males were extremely tall and muscular. Even just one of these humanoid robots would have cost a fortune.

"Wow!" Suzanne and Florence cried out together.

"This is my private collection," Ronald stated proudly.

Bradley and John stared at him, speechless.

"Did you build all these by yourself?" Ethan asked admiringly.

"It took me years; but yes, I did," replied Ronald.

Ronald then turned to a perfect lady figure behind him: she had shiny brown hair and attractive green eyes.

"This is Evelyn, my crown jewel," he introduced fondly. "My plan is to give her human thoughts to go with her human look. This way, Evelyn can fight Victor with us!"

"What?" Florence exclaimed, shooting Ronald an incredulous look as though she couldn't believe what she was hearing. "Please don't tell me you are creating a human-looking robot with human thinking, only for her to die in the fight against Victor!"

"Evelyn's not going to die," said Ronald defiantly as he caressed Evelyn's arm. "She's special. She's going to be brave, intelligent, and a real threat to Victor."

"So basically, your plan is to use Evelyn to fight Victor?" asked Bradley.

"No one will be used," Ronald answered sharply, "because I'll make sure Evelyn wants to fight. Needless to say, she'll be well-equipped."

"What about a robot army? Are you trying to create one?" asked John. He had been staring at the other robots in the cave.

"I wouldn't call it an army – it's more like a team," Ronald explained. "First, we need Evelyn, who can navigate the computer world better than any of us, to find out more about Victor. Then we need a few more … I'm thinking of muscular male robots … to help fight Victor in both the real world and computer world."

There was a short pause while the team of scientists considered Ronald's plan.

"One more question," said Florence. "Are we going to build the robots here, or in the factory?"

"Don't worry, I'll bring Evelyn to our London factory first thing tomorrow morning," Ronald replied with a smile. "Now, shall we get back to my house?"

Ronald led his team to the back of the cave. The elevator there took them back to Fischer Mansion. They made a stop at the wine cellar – an enviable private collection with racks of wines lined up according to age and origin.

"I think we deserve a few bottles for this special day –" said Ronald.

"Oh right, we almost forgot! Today's Ronald's birthday!"

Suzanne exclaimed.

"Yes, today's my birthday …" uttered Ronald, climbing up and down to pick the finest wines. "But more importantly, I want to remember it as the day we launch our big project – the creation of Evelyn, which will lead to the downfall of Victor …"

Afterwards, they followed Ronald into the dining room. As they stepped in, the ceiling screen dramatically brightened up from a bluish night to a sunny day. Six bar stools, which were stacked up in the corner, automatically unstacked themselves and scurried towards the bar table, ready to be sat on.

Ronald took out a selection of cheese and crackers to accompany their wines.

"Cheers everyone!" He raised his glass in a toast.

"Cheers!" the team of scientists shouted back.

They celebrated till late into the night. By the time they left Ronald's house in the Scottish Highlands, the wind had dropped a little. Further out, the sea was sparkling under the moonlight.

"Goodbye, see you all tomorrow!" Ronald waved at his team as their helicopter rose into the moonlit sky, diving into whirls of fast-moving clouds on this November night in year 2130.

CHAPTER 2

The Bodiless Head

When Evelyn opened her eyes in Stewart Corp's London factory two weeks later, all was dark. She felt like she had just woken up from a very long sleep. Unfortunately, she was still tired. She tried to fall back to sleep, but sleep evaded her.

Feeling restless, Evelyn snapped open her eyes suddenly: *Wow, this is a completely different place – it's full of sunshine here!* She had somehow landed in a computer simulation of the real world; she just knew it.

Are all parts of the computer world like this? Evelyn wondered excitedly.

She smiled. She was lying in a sweet green meadow, alone, and feeling perfectly at ease ... *Wait a moment, why's the Earth shaking?* Looking over her shoulder, Evelyn was surprised by what she saw: *Tigers* ... They were racing downhill with bared teeth, ready to maul her down!

Terrified, Evelyn jumped up from the meadow and ran towards the river. She froze at the sight of an enormous alligator, which was rising swiftly and silently out of the water ...

Evelyn instinctively squeezed her eyes shut. When she

opened her eyes again, she found herself back in the real world, which was a relief.

Evelyn checked her reflection in the glass in front: *What the hell is going on?* She screamed at the top of her voice as it dawned on her that she was just a helpless, naked head trapped inside a glass cupboard! She had got no legs, no arms, and no body or clothes.

At that moment, Evelyn heard footsteps. She stifled her screams and looked out of the glass cupboard anxiously. Six giants in laboratory gowns were entering the room – they were incredibly tall, but looked human enough.

"Gather around, everyone. Evelyn's awake!" one of the giants pointed a finger at her and shouted in a thrill voice. He was standing so close to Evelyn's eyes and ears that his finger looked like a tree trunk, and his voice shook her like thunder. Evelyn felt like an insect – tiny, insignificant, and in danger of being crushed to death by these giants.

The giants waved at each other. They came forward together, and quite unexpectedly, began to sing a birthday song to Evelyn:

"Happy birthday to you … Happy birthday to Evelyn …"

They clapped their hands too, which sounded so deafening to Evelyn it was as if someone was exploding fire crackers right next to her ears. But what bothered Evelyn the most was: *How do they know my name? Do I know them too?* She racked her brains – but no, she had absolutely no idea who these people were.

After they finished singing the song, one of the giants took a teddy bear from behind his back and put it right next to Evelyn. What a fright! The teddy bear was taller than Evelyn, and came in with such a draught it made Evelyn's head felt like rolling over. *Who says I want to sit next to a stuffed bear?* thought Evelyn grumpily.

As if the bear wasn't enough, the giants then took out a birthday cake, lighted the candle on top, and held the cake in front of Evelyn's face. The flickering flame was blinding; Evelyn blinked furiously. She wanted to sneeze too – taking a deep breath to calm her overstimulated senses, Evelyn was pleasantly surprised to find that the cake smelt sweet and delicious.

"Who are you?" she asked.

"My name's Ronald!" the giant standing nearest to her said proudly, taking off his thick-rimmed smartglasses to greet Evelyn in an ostentatious way. "I am the chief scientist, and this is my team."

He opened his arms in an embracing gesture to the five giants around him, then brought his arms back together and pointed at Evelyn with both thumbs.

Evelyn grimaced. All these sweeping movements from Ronald made her really dizzy. On top of that, she also had to worry about being knocked off the cupboard by him.

Seeing Evelyn's face, Ronald added smartly, "It must be boring sitting in the laboratory. Let's go for a walk!"

Evelyn's first thought was: *How?* She froze when she saw Ronald holding a glass box about the size of her head. The idea of being carried around by these giants sent a chill down her spine.

"Wait, no!" she shouted in horror, but Ronald had already wrapped his enormous hands around her head, which muffled her voice.

Ronald placed her head into the padded glass box, then closed the lid carefully. He clutched the box firmly in front of his chest and began to walk out of the laboratory. It wasn't as uncomfortable as Evelyn had feared, though it certainly felt strange to be carried around like a goldfish.

While Ronald walked to the door, Evelyn peered through the glass at the laboratory around. It was a clean and brightly lit place, with lots of computers and monitoring screens – she could hear the ceaseless humming and whirring of machines even in her box. There were also plenty of cupboards for storing robot parts. Evelyn quickly glanced into the cupboards, expecting to find heads like hers sitting on shelves, but there weren't any.

It was only a short walk before they entered another room. Space exploration seemed to be the theme here. Evelyn could see huge, alien-looking rocks hanging from the ceiling. There were numerous framed photos on the walls featuring droids, rovers, satellites and other space technology. Her gaze fell upon a huge space shuttle model displayed in an acrylic case – there were the words "TT Stewart Corporation" written on the shuttle's fuselage.

Ronald carefully removed Evelyn's head from the glass box and placed her on the sofa. He then sat on the floor opposite her. *This feels odd,* thought Evelyn.

"What's TT Stewart Corporation?" she asked, breaking the awkward silence.

"It's a company that specialises in making robots," Ronald answered, his expression frank and sincere. "Right now, you're in Stewart Corp's London factory."

"What am I doing here?" Evelyn wondered aloud.

"Well, since we are scientists, we like to create things – and so we created you," said Ronald, smiling warmly at her. He was obviously trying to be sensitive to Evelyn's feelings, but the news came as a shock to her anyway.

"You – created – me?" Evelyn uttered with astonished disbelief.

"Yes, I did, with my team." Ronald looked proud of himself.

Evelyn swallowed. The strange thing was, she didn't feel like something created in a laboratory … she felt fairly human, probably as human as a bodiless person could ever feel.

"Does that mean I'm a robot?" Evelyn asked, struggling to keep her voice steady. She was certain the answer would be yes, regardless of how she felt about herself …

"No, you are not a robot," Ronald said without hesitation.

"I'm not?" Evelyn was confused.

"We created you to be a human. Therefore, you are a human," Ronald told her simply.

"A human … without a body?" asked Evelyn, completely bewildered. "Did something go wrong?"

"No, everything's going according to plan. It's safer this way," Ronald answered in a brusque manner.

"What?" Evelyn exclaimed, raising her voice. "You knew I would wake up like this?"

"Look, we'll build you a body soon enough –"

"When?" Evelyn blurted out. She really wanted to shout at Ronald – for being selfish, inconsiderate, cold-blooded … for knowingly putting her into such misery.

"As early as tomorrow," said Ronald, gazing at Evelyn. "Look on the bright side – you don't live as a bodiless head every day. This kind of thing happens only once in a lifetime."

Evelyn stared at him, speechless.

The next day, Evelyn looked out of the glass cupboard

longingly. Through the windows of the laboratory, she could see the sun rose up, and then went down, but none of the scientists showed up that day.

Evelyn felt very anxious. She wondered whether Ronald had changed his mind about building her a human body. The idea that she could be stuck in this glass cupboard forever was unbearable. Evelyn forced herself to think positive: *He's coming tomorrow … of course he's coming …*

And she was right.

The following day, the sky had yet to fully brighten up when Ronald and two other scientists barged into the laboratory. Evelyn, who had been dozing lightly, jerked awake. She smiled broadly, ready for the morning greetings – which never came. Her heart sank when the scientists completely ignored her. They were speaking among themselves and dashing around the laboratory as if Evelyn didn't exist at all!

After about fifteen minutes, Ronald finally came to speak to her, "Right, Evelyn, we're almost ready. Just to let you know, we're going to put you to sleep mode while we build your body."

"Where have you been yesterday?" Evelyn asked him. She was seething inwardly, but managed to keep her tone quite casual.

"We've been extremely busy," Ronald said flatly. "I'm sorry to keep you waiting."

Evelyn's instinct was to shout at him. But she held her tongue, with difficulty … *This is not the time to be angry with Ronald, not when he is about to build me a human body.*

"How long is the process going to take?" she asked.

"About three hours, including testing and finalising."

"What are the chances of success?"

"Chances!" Ronald laughed. "We don't take chances. Trust

me, everything's going to turn out just fine."

When Evelyn regained consciousness, she found herself lazing in a rocking chair. She rocked herself to and fro absent-mindedly. Her memories came flooding back: last time she was awake, she was still a bodiless head, and Ronald said he was going to build her a human body …

Evelyn immediately looked at herself. She was amazed to find that she not only had a body – a nice and curvy one – she was also dressed in a purple silk dress. She double-checked: *Yes, I'm not imagining things. I've got a body and some pretty clothes.*

"Hooray!" Evelyn squealed with delight, clapping her hands and jumping up into the air.

Ronald, who was sitting in a rocking chair next to her, leapt up in alarm.

"Stop!" he shouted tensely. "Evelyn, you must follow my instructions."

Instructions! thought Evelyn as she burst out laughing. She had just reached a milestone in her life, and she wasn't going to spoil this special moment with instructions.

"How long have I been in sleep mode?" she asked excitedly.

"Three hours in the laboratory, and another hour here in the production hall," Ronald replied, watching her closely.

"The production hall?" Evelyn repeated to herself, puzzled.

They were in the control room on the top floor of the factory. Evelyn rushed to the side and looked down through the glass wall – "Oh my goodness!"

The production hall was gigantic, and the machines were beast-like. The whole place was illuminated by mysterious blue lights. Evelyn could see conveyor belts transporting metal parts and packed boxes to different levels of the production hall. Working on-site was a completely robotic workforce. The robots were dashing around on foot or in electric cars.

"Would you like a quick tour?" Ronald asked her.

Evelyn nodded. "Definitely!"

He led her out of the control room, across a short bridge and into a glass elevator, where he pressed the "down" button.

The elevator descended slowly. Evelyn winced: the heat and noise around her was quite unbearable. She could see red hot steel flowing in sturdy transparent pipes across the hall, tumbling like mini waterfalls at various places, causing white smoke to rise up and hang around. Meanwhile, metal slabs were being pounded into different shapes by enormous metal hammers, the thumping sounds were so loud they shook the whole hall. Looking more carefully, Evelyn could also see robot parts being churned out at incredible speed: metal arms, legs, joints …

"Do you like this place?" asked Ronald as the elevator continued its descent. He seemed to be enjoying himself.

Not wanting to disappoint Ronald, Evelyn was going to say yes, but stopped short. She had just spotted something very interesting below them: a door glowing in red – red laser beams were directed onto the door, creating a forbidding barrier.

"Ronald, what dangerous stuff are you keeping in there?" Evelyn asked jokingly, pointing at the glowing red door. "Nuclear weapons perhaps?"

Ronald didn't find her funny at all.

"That room's locked," he replied coldly, his face darkening all of a sudden, "let's get out of here."

Evelyn stared at him, astounded. *What is Ronald trying to hide from me?*

As their glass elevator reached the same level as the glowing red door, Evelyn focused her mind on that forbidding room. Then, most unexpectedly –

"Ouch!" Evelyn exclaimed, clutching her head. She thought she had just been "*zapped*" – it felt like an electric shock, and she was sure it came from that forbidding room.

For a brief moment, Evelyn considered telling Ronald about the *zap*. Then she pouted: *No, he won't believe me. He'll say I'm crazy.*

Ronald took Evelyn to one of the guest rooms in the factory and told her to stay.

"I'll be back tomorrow," he said and hurried off.

Evelyn tumbled into bed and tried to rest, but soon grew restless. Her mind was racing: the *zap*, Ronald, the forbidding room … *What's Ronald up to?*

There was no way Evelyn could stay still in this room. She jumped out of bed, dashed towards the door and set off for the production hall immediately. Along the way, she listened for signs of Ronald and his team, but they weren't working in this part of the factory. Harder to avoid was the robotic workforce. Running down the corridor, Evelyn passed a team of robots scanning and tagging packed boxes, and another team loading the boxes onto self-driving trucks. At first, Evelyn was worried these robots might be eyes for Ronald, but she soon noticed they were focusing solely on the task at hand and didn't care about anything else.

When Evelyn arrived at the production hall, it was as hot and noisy as before, but the mysterious blue lights had been switched off. Evelyn could barely see at first, but adjusted quickly: she realised she had night vision like cats.

Evelyn glanced up at the forbidding room – the glowing red door looked more tempting than ever in the darkness. She sprinted up the stairs, stopping outside the door. The *zap* in her head was back, and there was something else – she could feel something evil hiding behind those doors …

Ronald said the room's locked, Evelyn recalled. For a split second, she narrowed her eyes to concentrate on the glowing red door; then off she went, gathering speed and crashing into the room with all her might!

The door swung open violently. The alarms started blaring, but Evelyn ignored the noise. She turned her head just in time to see a puff of purple gas hanging in the corner of the room. Next second, the strongest *zap* she had ever experienced hit her – it was no longer just an electric shock, but felt as though an electric current was passing right through her head. The pain that came with it was so intense it made her head felt like exploding.

Evelyn shut her eyes tightly and screamed at the top of her lungs.

CHAPTER 3

The Yin-Yang Drones

It took a while for the pain to subside, then Evelyn opened her eyes ... *What? Not again!*

She was back in the computer world, alone, lying in the sweet green meadow. Evelyn shivered as she recalled the tigers and alligator that could jump out at any moment. *I've got to find another place,* she told herself. Leaping up from the grass, she started to run.

Evelyn was dashing uphill when she sensed waves in the air – someone was tracking her with sonar and radar signals. Next, she heard the flapping wings of insects. Evelyn stopped running and looked up: three beetle drones were hovering above her head. They had cameras for eyes and micro sensors covering their bodies. The patterns on their stomachs were most peculiar ... a circle divided by a curved line ... fiery red on one half, calming blue on the other ... with two dots near the centre. After a few seconds, Evelyn recognised it: this was the symbol of yin-yang, the Chinese philosophical belief on the balancing of opposite forces, except that the traditional black and white design had been replaced by more eye-catching colours.

Evelyn wondered what these yin-yang beetles were doing in the computer world. *Are they trying to tell me something?* She had a good feeling about them though – a feeling that they were sent by a potential friend.

The beetles were now flying away. Evelyn chased after them, hoping they would lead her to her new friend …

Ronald's furious voice stopped her in her tracks. He was yelling at her from the factory.

"Get up, Evelyn!"

Evelyn jerked awake. She was back in the forbidding room, sprawled on the floor. A furious Ronald and his team were towering over her. She quickly stood up.

"What are you doing in my private chamber?" Ronald demanded.

Evelyn looked around: the room was a complete mess. Lots of expensive-looking scientific instruments had fallen from their shelves and crashed to the ground – shattered. *Oh my God, what have I done?*

"I didn't mean to damage anything," she tried to explain, "I saw some purple gas. Next thing I knew, I was in the computer world."

"You saw some purple gas?" Ronald asked quietly. There was a dramatic change in his tone – he sounded unnerved.

"That's right, the purple gas was hanging there," said Evelyn, pointing at the corner of the room, "and my head felt like exploding –"

"Enough!" Ronald interrupted her. He turned to his team. "Florence, Ethan, would you take Evelyn to the observation room?"

Florence came forward, grabbed Evelyn roughly by the arms, and started to drag her out of Ronald's private chamber. Ethan marched beside them warily, like a prison guard.

Evelyn felt humiliated. "I'm just telling the truth!" she shouted, and let out an anguished wail. But Florence and Ethan simply carried on marching her out of the door, oblivious to her distress.

The observation room was completely different from the guest room. It was designed for holding robots, with security cameras mounted on the walls. *Ronald said I'm a human. How dare he treat me like a robot now!* thought Evelyn, feeling a jolt of shock and anger rushed through her.

Ronald and his team were in the corridor outside the observation room. Evelyn strained her ears to catch what they were saying:

"I've been enticing Victor to my private chamber lately … to analyse him more closely," Ronald was telling his team.

"Was Victor in your chamber then?" Florence asked impatiently. "Evelyn said she saw some purple gas; I've heard similar stories … about people seeing strange gases during or right after Victor's attacks."

"It means Victor had just left my chamber," Ronald answered calmly. "This has actually happened a few times. One moment my instruments are detecting plenty of Victor's activities, then boom – Victor is nowhere to be found."

"Evelyn also said her head felt like exploding," Suzanne chimed in eagerly. "Have any of you heard of that too, or did Evelyn just make that up?"

"No, I haven't," Florence admitted.

"But she's probably telling the truth," said Ronald, exhaling deeply. "Victor's presence tends to interfere with the electronics in my chamber, and we all know what Evelyn's head is made of."

"Metal and electronics …" muttered Suzanne.

"The point is," said Ronald authoritatively, "now that Victor has seen her, Evelyn must leave. This is for her own safety, and also for the security of the factory."

There was a murmur of agreement from his team of scientists.

Evelyn was leaning on the door, anxious to hear where she was headed, when the door burst open suddenly and Ronald barged in. She stumbled backwards but narrowly avoided falling.

"Next time, stay away from the door," Ronald told her unapologetically. "Come, Evelyn, we're getting out of here – now!"

Evelyn stared at him.

"To where?" she asked, not moving at all.

"Just follow me!" said Ronald irritably.

Evelyn followed Ronald out of the factory. It was cold and windy out in the open. She took a deep breath, looked up at the cloudy sky, and stretched her arms and legs … *Hmm, this feels liberating.*

Ronald ushered her to the parking lot: "Let's get into my car."

Evelyn gasped. Ronald's race car was in a league of its own – fully armoured, highly streamlined, and equipped with powerful wheels – not unlike Batman's car.

"I'm driving," he said once they were inside.

"Why?" Evelyn blurted out. "Aren't all cars self-driving these days?"

"Because we can't trust the autopilot system anymore," Ronald replied in a low voice. He started the car engine, drove out of the factory compound, and sped along the highway without another word.

The roaring of the race car engine was very satisfying to the senses, and for a while, Evelyn was able to forget all her worries in the world. But the carefree feeling didn't last long.

"Ronald, where exactly are we going?" she asked.

"To the London Cyber Hub," he said casually. "First trip, huh?"

"Why are we going there?"

"The London Cyber Hub is a really nice place … plenty of entertainment … there are bars, casinos, gaming centres …" he answered absent-mindedly.

"We're leaving the factory because of Victor, aren't we?" Evelyn cut in, gazing at Ronald with unblinking eyes.

"Well … yes, we are," Ronald answered slowly, looking more serious now.

"Tell me about him and his attacks."

"I wonder how much you already know," said Ronald, looking thoughtful. "To put it simply, Victor's attacks around the world are now reaching crisis point. So far, the authorities have yet to come up with an effective plan to fight back. Everyone's in danger, especially you –"

They had just left the highway and were entering central London when a security device in the car started beeping loudly.

"We are being followed," said Ronald. He tensed up and concentrated on the road ahead, swerving left and right in a bid to shake off their followers.

Evelyn glanced at Ronald's monitoring screen and saw that a silver car was on their tail. This was hardly the first time she was being followed. Feeling more curious than nervous, Evelyn lowered the window and looked out. She was hoping to catch a glimpse of the faces of their followers, but instead, she found something hovering outside the window – beetle drones … the same three yin-yang beetle drones she had seen in the computer world. Evelyn held out her hand and tried to catch one of the beetles, but it simply flew higher and avoided her grasp, which was disappointing. She peered at the traffic behind to see what the silver car was up to, only to find that it was no longer on their tail – Ronald must have lost it. Wind was rushing in fiercely, so Evelyn raised the car window.

"Three beetle drones have caught up with us," she told Ronald.

"Insects," Ronald muttered dismissively, "not a problem."

He swerved left into a quiet residential street, then pressed the acceleration button – immediately, their car roared and sped forward. Taking a wide turn as they reached the end of the street, Ronald pressed the acceleration button again and off they went.

Evelyn pressed her nose against the window and looked through it: the yin-yang beetles were gone. Ronald's monitoring screen showed that the silver car had left the road and came to a halt.

"See, they have already given up!" Ronald declared triumphantly. "They know their car is no match for mine. We've won."

"Oh," Evelyn uttered. "Do you know who our followers are?"

"Whoever they are, I dare say our followers are up to no good!" said Ronald, raising his voice.

Evelyn stared at him: Ronald's face had turned red. He looked angry.

"Don't worry," Ronald added. "Once we're in London Cyber Hub, we'll be safe."

"Why?" asked Evelyn.

"Because drones go crazy inside," Ronald answered matter-of-factly. "There are too many electronic distractions. They won't be able to track us."

They came to a stop on a bustling street lined with bars, hotels and a cinema. Stepping out of the car, Evelyn was bombarded by advertisements that jumped out of their light boxes to tout for business. She found herself surrounded by holographic projections of a bar girl, a hotel concierge, and a team of comic-book superheroes. There was also a map that showed all the shops and entertainment venues at the London Cyber Hub.

Evelyn went on to read the map excitedly. She was wondering where to start first when Ronald grabbed her arm.

"Come, let's get to the bar. I need a drink," he said roughly.

Evelyn shook her head. *He knows I don't drink.*

"I'm going to wait outside while you get your drink –"

Ronald shot her a sharp glance.

"Don't wander off! You're coming with me to the bar," he told her, his expression stern.

Evelyn followed Ronald to The Time Traveller: customers had to walk through a "time tunnel" – filled with dazzling lights – before entering the bar. Coming out of the tunnel, Evelyn felt like she had travelled back in time. The bar was very spacious, and had a nostalgic setting. Evelyn could see classic pinball machines, pool tables, vintage jukeboxes … Ronald ordered a glass of champagne from the barmaid and settled down at a quiet corner with Evelyn. He drank, burped, then drank again …

There was a live performance on stage. Evelyn could see humans and robots dancing side by side. Amused, she craned her neck to get a better view. *Aaah, why's my neck so stiff?*

Something was not right – Evelyn felt as though she was covered with a swarm of flies. She quickly looked around, but couldn't see any fly, which was creepy! *They must be invisible to the human eye,* she thought, activating her enhanced vision to look again.

Now she could see them: clinging to her clothes were thousands of nano robots. They were extremely tiny and resembled specks of dust. *Do they have the yin-yang symbol too?* she wondered, but it was impossible to tell because these robots were too tiny.

Evelyn tried to brush them off with her fingers – she couldn't. The nano robots had an incredibly tenacious grip on her clothes. Growing impatient, Evelyn began to twitch and twist, as vigorously as the dancers on stage, in an attempt to shake the nano robots off her clothes.

"Is everything all right?" Ronald shouted at her.

"I can do it," Evelyn mumbled. She was too busy right now to explain to Ronald about the robots that his human eyes couldn't see.

Ronald frowned and took out a device that looked like a remote control with antennas.

"Beep, beep, beep!" Warning sounds blared out of the device as soon as he switched it on.

"We are leaving!" Ronald announced. He grabbed Evelyn's arm and rushed to the back door with her.

Ronald pulled Evelyn aside once they were outside the bar.

"Listen, Evelyn, it's probably Victor who's after you. He and his evil accomplices may even be listening to us as we speak."

What? thought Evelyn, aghast. She had a rather strong feeling that it was the "yin-yang clan", not Victor, who was after her. She was quite sure her followers were friendly too, because if they had meant to harm her, they would have done it by now.

"In any case, it's time for you to weapon up," Ronald added urgently.

"I beg your pardon!" Evelyn exclaimed, incredulous.

"I said it's time for you to weapon up," Ronald repeated, without batting an eyelid.

"How?"

"I'm going to unlock your special firing system. All you have to do is listen to my instructions and destroy all the nano robots on your body."

In spite of Ronald's sensible tone, Evelyn was under no illusion what he was trying to do: *To manipulate me, control me … make me his tool, his puppet!*

"Why would I do that?" Evelyn asked, fuming. "Do you know who our followers are?"

"As I've told you, my guess –"

"Guess!" Evelyn cried, her voice shaking with rage. "Before you decide to kill thousands of robots indiscriminately, don't you think the least you can do is to find out who sent them?"

"Calm down, Evelyn," Ronald yelled at her, exasperated. "No one is going to be killed. These are just robots –"

"Just robots!" Evelyn bellowed hysterically.

They glared at each other. Evelyn stepped away from Ronald.

"I'm disgusted," she spat. "I'm not like you; I don't kill indiscriminately – so leave me alone!"

Turning her back on him, Evelyn stormed across the street and started running. She could hear Ronald shouting behind her, his tone crazed and wild: "Don't be naïve, Evelyn, your body's full of Victor's robots! If you don't destroy them now, Victor's going to capture and torture you …"

CHAPTER 4

The Kung Fu Headmaster

Evelyn kept running. She had no idea where she was going, nor how far she had gone – not that she cared. Right now, she just wanted to get as far away from Ronald as possible. She shuddered at the thought of him. *That robot-killing maniac …*

Evelyn ran on and on, focusing purely on the sensation of speed. It was a liberating sensation. She was just beginning to feel better when a man's voice materialised out of nowhere.

"Stop!" he shouted at her, his voice deep, reverberating and filled with menace. "You, stop right there!"

Evelyn ran even faster – of course she wasn't going to stop. Someone was clearly after her though, and she felt nervous. She had to keep telling herself: *I'm not afraid of you, I'm not afraid of you … Catch me if you can!*

A shadow flitted past her, halting right in front of her to block her way. Evelyn didn't see it coming. She ran into it headlong – *Ouch!* The shadow turned out to be solid, like a mountain, and absolutely unmovable.

Evelyn looked up, then began to shake from head to toe uncontrollably. In front of her was a giant of a man wearing all black. Not only was he tall and muscular, but he was also pointing an electric gun at her neck, ready to shoot her at point-blank range!

Definitely not friendly, thought Evelyn, feeling doomed.

"Don't move," the man commanded in a tense yet authoritative voice.

He approached her cautiously. With one hand still pointing the electric gun at Evelyn's neck, he used his other hand to wave a portable scanner an inch away from her body. He was scanning her in a fast and fluid way. No one told Evelyn what to expect; but somehow, she just knew that if the scanner went "beep, beep, beep", she would be a dead girl in no time. She prayed that everything would stay silent.

"You may go," the man said suddenly, ending her ordeal as abruptly as it started. The menace in his voice was gone, and he sounded almost friendly.

The man shoved both his electric gun and portable scanner into his bag. He then took out a silver case the size of a wallet – engraved upon the case was the same yin-yang sign which Evelyn had seen on the beetle drones.

What? thought Evelyn, *it was him, following me?* She watched in amazement as the nano robots that had been clinging to her body lost interest in her all of a sudden and flew back into the case. The man then shut the case with a click and shoved that into his bag too.

Evelyn cast a searching glance up at the man's face. It struck her that he looked young and radiant. He had an intelligent face, black hair, and bright blue eyes that stood out strikingly.

"Who are you?" she asked, completely baffled.

The man peered directly into Evelyn's eyes.

"My name's Guillermo. I'm the headmaster of Yin-Yang Martial Arts University," he said, his voice loud and clear.

Evelyn snorted: *This man … headmaster? There's probably no such thing as a Martial Arts University!*

"Crazy!" she blurted out. Remembering how he had pointed a gun at her neck merely minutes ago, Evelyn took flight immediately. She sprinted down street after street, never once looking back, feeling just happy to be alive.

When Evelyn slowed down at last, the sky was getting dark. She found herself in another part of London Cyber Hub. Apart from bars, there wasn't much else in sight. This didn't bother Evelyn. What really bothered her was the fact that despite sprinting down ten streets in a row, it was impossible for her to shake off the image of that self-proclaimed headmaster from her mind. She decided to search for information about him on the Internet, just to put her mind at rest.

Evelyn couldn't believe what she found out. *Good heavens, there really exists a Yin-Yang Martial Arts University on the planet!* Located in Sichuan Province of China, the University was founded by a visionary called Master Chow, and the current headmaster was none other than Master Guillermo! On Headmaster's Page, Evelyn could see a muscular young man dressed smartly in Chinese martial arts robe, his bright blue eyes glittering with a strong sense of purpose … and he had very hairy arms.

Evelyn was thunderstruck. For a moment, she was seriously tempted to dash back and have a chat with Guillermo – to say sorry for misjudging him, at the very least. Then she changed her mind. *Don't be stupid,* she scolded herself, *he would have left by now.*

Evelyn had barely finished searching about Guillermo when she heard men calling out to her: "Baby!" … "Princess!" … "Sweetie!" … These were followed by obnoxious kissing sounds and whistlings.

Evelyn ignored them all.

"Drunks!" she muttered with contempt and walked on.

A few seconds later, Evelyn heard wobbling footsteps behind her. A man reeking of alcohol had come up to her. He was grinning devilishly and holding a glass bottle. As the man raised his arm to hit Evelyn with the glass bottle, Evelyn reacted instinctively: she jumped up and delivered a back kick right at his stomach. The man threw up instantly, then fell to the ground clutching his stomach.

Seeing what Evelyn did to their companion, the other drunks grew wild with rage. There were five men, who growled and went on kicking, punching and swinging wine bottles at Evelyn. Evelyn defended herself with ease: fighting was like her second nature, and she knew exactly where to aim and how hard to hit.

All went well until Evelyn heard ominous crackling sounds. She jerked her head around and was aghast to find herself looking into the firing end of an electric gun: one of them was armed! Laughing maniacally, the armed man wasted no time to fire into her throat. The searing pain that ensued was unlike anything Evelyn had felt before. It immobilised her. *Now I'm like a rag doll, at the mercy of these drunks …*

They showed no mercy. Dragging Evelyn on the concrete pavement, these men kicked and punched her over and over again. Blinding pain shot through Evelyn's entire body. She screamed for help, but her voice was drowned out by the evil laughter of her attackers.

At that moment, someone stabbed her with a broken glass bottle. Illuminated by the street light above her, Evelyn saw red blood gushing out of her skin and flesh. She was in shock, and felt numb. Tears were pouring out of her eyes, blurring her vision … when all of a sudden, the drunks stopped punching and kicking her. *How strange*, thought Evelyn, as she struggled to peer out of her teary eyes.

At first, Evelyn thought she saw a knight coming to her rescue. She blinked, and as her vision cleared up, she realised it was Guillermo, the headmaster of Yin-Yang Martial Arts University whom she met earlier.

The sight of Guillermo was a painkiller in itself: Evelyn already felt better! She watched in awe as Guillermo raised his mighty leg to sweep across her attackers – they fell like bowling pins, but got back on their feet after a while, yelling, growling, clearly unwilling to give up.

The man with an electric gun suddenly raised his weapon, but Guillermo was faster than him. The man found his own gun knocked to the ground, and he was also facing an electric gun which was longer, bigger, and obviously more powerful than his. He and his companions fled in terror at once, scampering down dark alleys like rats.

Putting his electric gun away, Guillermo stepped forward and squatted down beside Evelyn.

"We meet again!" cried Evelyn, thrilled.

Guillermo sighed. "They shouldn't have attacked you. How are you feeling?"

"Um … pretty awful," she answered truthfully.

"Can you move?" he asked.

"No, I can't," she groaned.

"Would you like me to have a look?" he asked politely.

"Yes, please!" she said without hesitation.

Guillermo nodded, edging closer to survey her for injury.

"You've dislocated a few joints of the arms and legs," he told her in a deep, calm voice. "Would you like me to fix them now?"

"Oh, yes," she responded eagerly.

While Guillermo pulled her arms and legs into position, Evelyn decided this was the perfect opportunity to start some small talk.

"What brings you here?" she asked, trying to sound casual. "Did you come to have a glass of wine?"

"I don't drink," he told her sternly.

"Of course you don't, Master Guillermo."

Guillermo shot a sharp glance at her. "So you checked?"

"Ow!" Evelyn yelped as the first dislocated joint was put back in place. "Yes, I checked, but I can't find everything. Guillermo, how old are you exactly?" she asked curiously.

"That's not the point." He was stern again.

"Anyway, I read that you started learning martial arts at the tender age of six, which means you've got loads of fighting experience under your belt," Evelyn praised.

"Thanks for the compliment." He sounded nonchalant. "What's your name, by the way?"

"My name's Evelyn." She beamed at him.

Guillermo continued to fix Evelyn's joints. "Ouch, Ouch, Ouch!" she exclaimed as the rest of her dislocated joints were put back in place one by one. After that, Evelyn felt much better.

"Thank you," she said gratefully. Now she could walk, but her face was still bleeding.

"You're welcome. As for your face, I've got antiseptics, bandages and other first-aid supplies in my hotel room – it's just three minutes' drive from here." He paused and pointed at one of the bigger bars behind them. "You can wait in that bar while I retrieve my supplies. I'll talk to the owner there. You should be safe inside." He turned and began to walk towards the bar.

"Look, Guillermo, if you don't mind, I can go with you to the hotel – to save time," Evelyn said hastily as she walked beside him. "Perhaps you can also treat my injuries in your room instead of out here," she added hopefully.

Guillermo jerked his head at Evelyn. Then, sounding like a strict father, he lectured her, "You are a girl. It's not good to get into a man's car or his room alone the first time you meet him."

"But I'm a different kind of girl!" Evelyn argued, red-faced. "You know I've got a metal core under my skin and flesh, which makes me a bit different."

Guillermo hesitated … frowning slightly, he relented.

"Fine, you've got a point. Follow me." He helped Evelyn into his car, which swiftly drove them out of the Cyber Hub.

"Where are you staying in London?" Evelyn asked him.

"The Homely and Cosy," he replied, looking relaxed. "It's one of the few independent hotels left in the city. The rest are all owned by Stewart Corp now."

"I see," Evelyn murmured. She wondered what Guillermo would think of her if he knew she was created in a Stewart Corp factory.

Three minutes later, they were in front of the hotel. Standing ten storeys high with a traditional red brick design, the Homely and Cosy looked quite insignificant compared to the magnificent commercial buildings around it. It did, however, seem like a nice warm place to spend the night.

The car drove itself to the underground car park. Once parked, it asked, "Would you like to return this vehicle, sir?"

Guillermo pressed a few keys on the navigation screen. "Let's go," he said. Evelyn followed him into the elevator.

Guillermo's room was located on the top floor. It was a business suite. He opened the door for her. Evelyn stepped inside and was immediately greeted by a huge mahogany desk with matching office stationery on it.

Guillermo guided her through the office into the living room. Pointing at a black leather sofa, he said politely, "Please sit. I'll be back in a moment."

He went into the bathroom and closed the door. When he came out again, he was carrying a full tray of first-aid equipment. There was a basin of water, some clean towels, an antiseptic spray, and a disposable stitching pack – "specially designed for human skin, needle and threads included". Evelyn winced: she hated needles.

Guillermo sat beside Evelyn and started dabbing her wounds with a wet towel. Evelyn felt tiny beside this gentle giant.

"I shudder to think what could have happened to you. How dare those men beat you up like this?" he said, his brow furrowed.

Evelyn blushed. Speaking of the incident, she could clearly remember how the men were catcalling at her. But what stood out even more vividly in her mind was how, minutes before the attack, she had been taken aback by the revelation about Guillermo's true identity, awestruck by his status as headmaster, and mesmerised by the photo of him in Chinese martial arts robe …

"They were harassing me. I guess they attacked me because I ignored them," she said feebly.

Guillermo changed to a clean towel and continued dabbing

Evelyn's bloody face.

"I want to know more about you," he said gently. "Have you always got this metal core inside your body?"

"Actually, when I first woke up, I was just a head," Evelyn answered frankly.

"I'm sorry," Guillermo muttered.

"Then my creator built me this body. His name's Ronald, by the way –"

Guillermo looked up at her, his eyes alight with interest.

"It's complicated." She shrugged.

"Tell me about it," said Guillermo. He peered into Evelyn's face and began spraying her wounds with antiseptics and anaesthetics, which numbed her skin.

"I ran away from Ronald."

"Why? Was he abusive?" Guillermo asked, furrowing his brow.

"No, Ronald didn't abuse me. It's worse – he's a robot killer!" Evelyn said in disgust.

"What happened?"

"He doesn't care … he doesn't bother to check. He's quick to kill any robot that seems evil in his eyes!" Evelyn ranted, feeling emotional. "If one morning he wakes up and thinks I'm evil, I'll be dead by midday!"

"That's unfair. No wonder you ran away from him," Guillermo murmured, shaking his head. "Did Ronald ever mention why he created you?"

"No, we never discussed that," Evelyn answered, still upset. "But I've got a special firing system – Ronald tried to activate it just before I ran away – so I guess he intended me to be a fighter of some sort."

"That explains a lot," said Guillermo. He tore open the

stitching pack, ready to stitch up Evelyn's wounds. Looking into the sharp end of the needle, Evelyn flinched. She jerked her head away just as the needle was about to pierce into her face, leaving Guillermo's hand hanging in mid-air.

Guillermo cocked his head to one side, amused.

"Don't worry, it won't hurt. I've already sprayed you with anaesthetics," he said, smiling knowingly at her.

Evelyn watched warily as the needle penetrated her skin: once, twice … it was best not to keep count.

"That should heal in fifteen minutes," Guillermo told her as he finally put the needle away.

It struck Evelyn that they were about to say goodbye. Evelyn didn't want to go yet – *Guillermo seems like a nice and decent man. We can be friends.* Besides, where was she supposed to go now that she had left Ronald?

And then, a thought crossed Evelyn's mind. She took a deep breath.

"Guillermo, would you tell me more about Yin-Yang Martial Arts University?" she asked, gazing at him with wide, sparkling eyes. "It sounds like a really interesting and unusual school, and you are the headmaster!"

Guillermo ran a finger through his jet-black hair.

"It's the finest martial arts school and the only martial arts university in the world," he said, looking very sincere. "We have aspiring students coming from all over the world. The school is founded by Master Chow, a formidable expert in both martial arts and computer science."

"Is Master Chow your teacher?" Evelyn asked intuitively.

Guillermo gazed fixedly at Evelyn with his blue eyes and said, "Not only is he my teacher, he also knows your creator."

"You mean Master Chow knows Ronald?" Evelyn cried out in surprise.

Guillermo nodded. "They used to work in the same team in TT Stewart Corporation as computer scientists, but parted ways ten years ago: Master Chow went on to become the founder of Yin-Yang Martial Arts University, while Ronald continued to work for Stewart Corp."

Evelyn's mouth dropped open. *What a revelation!*

"There's something else I need to ask you," Guillermo went on. "Evelyn, did Ronald ever talk to you about Victor?"

"Yes," Evelyn answered nervously, "he said Victor's attacks around the world are now reaching crisis point."

"Ronald's right," said Guillermo with a tense expression. "Victor's an evil computer virus that is currently lurking in the computer world – he's still new, and quite unstable. But it is our belief that Victor will soon acquire robot bodies in the real world to maximise his destructive power."

Evelyn's face turned pale. *Oh no.*

"Recently, Victor has been killing innocents to test his powers. Several computer experts have been murdered for trying to find and destroy Victor."

"Is Master Chow in danger? Are you in danger?" Evelyn asked quickly.

"We are safe for now," Guillermo reassured her in a soft voice. "The point is, Evelyn, it is our belief that Ronald has created you to fight Victor ... designing you in such a way that you can fight evils in the real world ... and also chase Victor in the computer world to eventually kill him off."

Evelyn sat stunned on the sofa. "Fight Victor ... me?" she muttered, utterly dumbfounded.

She glanced at Guillermo and saw that there was a sparkle in his eyes. *Is that the light of hope, that one day, I will kill off Victor for the whole world?*

She swallowed hard, and determinedly tore her eyes away from him.

"I think your wounds are healed now," Guillermo said suddenly, handing her a mirror. "Take a look for yourself."

Feeling self-conscious, Evelyn stared at herself in the mirror: her face was no longer bloody, and her skin looked smooth.

"Thank you for patching me up," said Evelyn, blushing under Guillermo's intense scrutiny. She stood up, but instantly dropped back to the sofa with a grimace … *That hurts!*

Guillermo regarded her sympathetically. "I see your body is still aching. Don't worry, we're going to Chinatown tomorrow to heal your aches."

He began cleaning up the sofa. Evelyn, meanwhile, forgot all about her pain. She felt as excited as a child before her school trip. *Yes! We're travelling to Chinatown tomorrow!*

"Guillermo, are you a computer expert too?" she asked cheerfully.

"Yes, I am," he said, with a bit of pride.

"And you intend to fight Victor, together with Master Chow?"

"Yes, definitely," he said firmly.

"That's very brave of you," Evelyn praised. "So how exactly do I fit into this grand scheme of yours and Master Chow's?"

"It remains to be seen," he said, his expression guarded.

Evelyn scowled. *That's vague!*

"Guillermo, did you come to London specifically to find me and tell me about Victor?" she asked directly.

"You can say that," he answered in a slightly husky voice. "It hasn't been easy to track you down. I'm sorry if I scared you at first."

They could hear the bells chiming from a nearby church – it was already midnight.

"Let's meet up again tomorrow morning," said Guillermo. "Where are you staying tonight, Evelyn?"

"To be honest, I haven't made any plans …"

"Would you like me to take you back to Ronald's factory?" he suggested. "You've got a room there, don't you?"

Evelyn shook her head petulantly. "Since it's really late now, if you don't mind, I'd rather spend the night in this room."

She peeked up at Guillermo and saw that he had raised his eyebrows –

"In this case, you may take my bed," he said simply.

"Where will you sleep?" Evelyn asked, surprised.

"I can sleep on the sofa." He gave a nonchalant shrug.

"Please don't let me keep you from sleeping," Evelyn said quickly. "I don't need to sleep anyway."

Guillermo's eyes softened, and he smiled slightly. "That's very considerate of you. I'll take the bed then. You may keep the lights on for the night."

"I don't need lights," Evelyn explained, "I can use my infrared eyes for night vision."

"All right, just make yourself at home," said Guillermo, giving her a doting smile.

Fifteen minutes later, Guillermo came out of the bathroom, freshly showered and ready for bed.

"Goodnight, Evelyn."

"Goodnight, Guillermo."

CHAPTER 5

Surprises in Chinatown

At first, Evelyn stayed on the sofa. She tried to pass the time recharging herself. Since she was not low on energy, it took a mere twenty minutes before this was completed. Next, she tried to update her internal programs, only to be notified that they were already fully up to date.

Peeping into the bedroom, Evelyn could see Guillermo sleeping soundly. The silence in the living room was unbearable. She missed him already, and was sorely tempted to rouse him for company. In the end, Evelyn decided to lie down on the sofa and put herself to sleep mode.

She slept on and on, until suddenly, she snapped open her eyes: the curtains had been pulled aside, allowing the room to bathe in the warm sunlight of this winter morning. For a moment, Evelyn was confused … *Where am I?* She looked around and saw a man standing next to the wardrobe, quickly putting on his t-shirt – he was tall, muscular and hairy.

Evelyn recognised him immediately. *This is Guillermo, headmaster of Yin-Yang Martial Arts University, the man who saved my life yesterday!* Suddenly, she was bursting with energy. She gazed admiringly up at Guillermo.

"Will you be practising martial arts this morning?" she asked, her eyes sparkling with anticipation. "I'd love to be your audience!"

Guillermo chuckled, "All right." In the blink of an eye, he had flipped himself upside down against the wall.

Evelyn gasped in amazement, "Wow!"

At first, Guillermo supported himself with both hands. He then stood on one hand and withdrew his fingers gradually, staying upside down with five fingers … three fingers … one finger. Evelyn watched in awe as Guillermo held himself upside down with just his thumb for an entire minute! After that, he agilely jumped back to his feet to stand in an upright position.

"The one-finger handstand," said Guillermo with a satisfied smile.

Evelyn stared at him. She had never seen anything like this. Guillermo's fingers were like steel: they didn't even shake while bearing the entire weight of his body.

Guillermo slung his bag over his shoulder. "Come," he called out to her, "we're going to Chinatown to heal your body aches."

Evelyn followed Guillermo out of the room into the elevator. As the elevator doors opened on the ground floor, she was pleased to see that the hotel lobby was bustling with activity: apart from human guests, there was also a band of robot musicians carrying heavy musical instruments, a few robot secretaries standing beside their well-dressed owners, and even a pet chimpanzee.

"Are all hotels these days so welcoming to – er – guests of different shapes and sizes?"

"Not all," said Guillermo, "but this one's known for its inclusiveness … Look, our car has arrived." He gestured to the driveway outside the hotel entrance.

Their "car" turned out to be an automatic open-top rickshaw. It looked traditional and elaborate, apparently designed for Chinese celebrations. Evelyn was impressed. She climbed in after Guillermo. As they sat side by side, Evelyn couldn't help but ask, "Why are we riding in something this slow?"

Guillermo smiled. "Don't be fooled by its appearance. This rickshaw is fast –"

He had barely finished his sentence when the rickshaw's engine started to roar like a lion. The next thing Evelyn knew, the rickshaw had jerked forward and was sprinting down the hotel driveway like a beast. *Whoa!* Evelyn was so shocked she had to hold on to Guillermo's muscular arm to steady herself.

The rickshaw was travelling so fast she could feel the strong, cold wind biting into her face. Evelyn turned her collar up against the wind, then cast a sidelong glance at Guillermo – he seemed totally unaffected by the elements. *Unbelievable!*

London's Chinatown was a famous cultural district surrounded by walls of red bricks. It looked magnificent. There was an artificial moat outside. White and grey swans could be seen lazing around in the icy water.

They entered through one of the stone arch bridges. Inside the red walls, it was bursting with life. As their rickshaw drove along the bustling street market, Evelyn felt a bombardment to her senses. Pet sparrows from a shop on their right were making such shrill, incessant cries that Evelyn had to clap her hands over her ears to shut out the noise … A condiment store on their left was brewing soy sauce so intense in smell it stank the entire street out … Meanwhile, colourful embroidered handbags were hanging in the balconies of various shops, looking absolutely delightful. Their rickshaw also drove past an antique shop with delicate porcelain vases lined up outside its door …

"See the surnames?" Guillermo pointed at one of the shop front signs. "Unlike those in central London, these shops are mainly owned by small businesses, named after the family who founded them –"

A boy and a girl suddenly ran onto the road, causing their rickshaw to brake hard! They waited while the children crossed the road.

"How do you pronounce the name 'Ng'?" Evelyn asked out of curiosity, pointing at a sign in front of them, which read "Ng's Locksmith Services: Expert in Locks Since 1995".

"That's a surname, and you say it with your nose instead of tongue: NG …" Guillermo demonstrated skilfully. "Same as the sound you make when the food tastes good."

Their beastly rickshaw picked up speed again. It took them all the way up to the western gate of Chinatown, stopping in front of a thick grove of bamboo trees.

"Are we meeting someone in this oriental garden?" Evelyn asked, hopping out of the rickshaw to stretch her arms and legs.

"This is not an oriental garden," Guillermo corrected her. "This is a shop, a very unique shop for healing. Follow me!"

They walked onto the cobblestone path, which wound its way through the tall bamboo trees. The trees were grown so close to each other they completely blocked out the sky, casting huge shadows on the ground. Along the path, there were alien-looking cactuses full of intimidating thorns, big red tantalising flowers that had attracted giant bees, and poisonous-looking mushrooms which were flourishing on the damp soil.

As Evelyn stared into a cluster of bright scarlet mushrooms, an old lady's voice with a Chinese accent announced in a diagnostic tone: "You've got pain in your head, shoulder, chest and legs. You've come to the right place."

Evelyn immediately looked up into the bamboo trees, but there were too many leaves and branches to spot the hidden speaker.

They had reached the end of the path. In front of them was a two-storey cottage. Two giant porcelain vases stood on either side of the oak front door like guards. There were elaborate carvings on the vases. On closer inspection, Evelyn found that the carvings were actually acupuncture charts which showed the thousands of acupuncture points on a human body …

It suddenly dawned on Evelyn that she was going to get acupuncture. A horrifying image came unbidden into her mind: it was the image of a lone warrior … being shot by thousands of arrows simultaneously fired by an enemy army … becoming a standing porcupine the next second … before collapsing to the ground and dying a painful death!

"I don't want to be punctured to death!" Evelyn screamed, losing control of herself completely.

She turned tail and ran away, knocking down a few bamboo shoots along the way.

"Stop!" Guillermo commanded, but it was too late. Evelyn had tripped over a decorative rock on the side of the path, falling facedown onto several big and spiky cactuses.

"Ahhhhhhhhh!" she wailed in agony as hundreds of cactus needles pierced her face all at once.

When Evelyn looked up, she found Guillermo already by her side, crouching beside her. His eyes were intense as he examined her face. Holding her close to his chest, he began pulling out the cactus needles one by one.

In the safety of Guillermo's warm body, Evelyn began to sob like an injured rabbit. Tears rolled down her face.

"I don't want acupuncture … I don't want to be punctured!" she said between sobs.

"Stay still," Guillermo ordered her, before adding in a softer voice, "who says you are getting acupuncture, by the way?"

Evelyn stopped sobbing. "I'm not?" she asked dazedly.

"No, you're not," said Guillermo, removing the last remaining cactus needles from Evelyn's face. "Here you go, you look good now."

He released Evelyn from his arm and led her back to the oak front door of the cottage. Standing between the two giant porcelain vases, he looked Evelyn in the eye and explained patiently, "I've brought you here for a treatment called Acu-Pressure – don't worry, there will be no needles, no punctures, and it won't hurt. Trust me!"

He opened the door for her.

Slowly, dragging her feet, Evelyn walked into the cottage. As soon as she set foot on the squeaky wooden floorboards, a strong pungent smell assaulted her nostrils and stung her eyes. Evelyn wrinkled her nose, while trying to blink back tears.

"What's that hideous smell?" she asked in a hoarse voice. She was quite certain that … somewhere here, there must be a witch brewing evil potions!

"This is where they keep their traditional Chinese medicine – strong and powerful stuff to swallow," came Guillermo's voice. "Obviously, you won't be needing them."

Evelyn instantly breathed a sigh of relief.

It took a while for Evelyn to adjust to the alien environment.

When she finally felt well enough to look around, she found herself in a dimly lit room, surrounded by jars and jars of strange objects – swimming, floating or simply bathing in their ominously coloured concoctions. Reading the labels curiously, Evelyn could see there were seahorses, black fungi, ginseng, scorpion stingers, spider legs …

Spider legs? A shiver ran down her spine. The jars were stacked to the ceiling, and there were hundreds if not a thousand of them.

"Are these jars airtight?"

"The medicines inside these jars are living things." Guillermo looked back at her knowledgeably. "There are holes in the lids to let them breathe."

"No wonder this place stinks," Evelyn muttered, contorting her face in disgust.

Guillermo led her through a corridor to a large, circular room: the healing chamber.

"Wow," Evelyn exclaimed. Unlike the room of Chinese medicine, this place actually felt nice and pleasant. There was a beautiful marble fountain at the centre with water shooting up from the top. The soft hypnotic sound of water splashing back down echoed throughout the circular chamber – Evelyn felt very relaxed instantly.

There were eight healing beds in the chamber, all fitted with futuristic nano-foam cushions. Stowed neatly under each bed were robotic arms capable of delivering high pressure, targeted air jets for the acupressure treatment. The beds looked divinely comfortable, and two were already occupied.

Evelyn laid down on one of the futuristic beds. It was so soothing: every part of her body – head, neck, back, arms and legs – was supported by the spongy nano-foam. Evelyn looked up at the ceiling … it was a screen, right now showing a night sky with countless twinkling stars. She almost fell asleep when the super soft sheet under her, which was green and looked like a lotus leaf, gradually curled up to cover her entire body.

"Ready?" a hypnotic female voice murmured into Evelyn's ear. "Here begins our journey into the deepest forests of wild China."

Wrapped inside the leaf-like sheet, Evelyn felt strong concentrated jets of air directed to specific acupressure points on her arms and legs. She relaxed and smiled. Next, she felt jets of air directed to her head, neck and chest. The pressure was just right, alternating rhythmically – faster, slower, sporadic, continuous … It was so relaxing that Evelyn felt lighter and lighter, until she was light as a feather, as though she was floating on layers of fluffy clouds up in the sky. Evelyn could still hear the sound of water from the fountain in the healing chamber, but now it sounded more like that of a waterfall … *A giant waterfall in the mountain forest below the clouds*, she imagined.

Evelyn let her imagination roam free:

She imagined a Great White Eagle flying next to her, flapping its muscular wings, inviting her to sit on its wide back. Evelyn stroked its snowy feathers, then climbed onto the eagle, her legs astride.

It's cold up here! She heard herself say between chattering teeth.

The eagle looked back in concern: Evelyn realised she was looking into Guillermo's face! He wrapped a broad, muscular wing around her – warmth instantly spread through Evelyn's entire body.

He was an excellent flyer. With Evelyn on his back, Guillermo the Eagle somersaulted skilfully, tumbled playfully, before soaring up and high again –

Whoa, Guillermo! Evelyn cheered. In response, the eagle patted her gently with his broad wings.

There were just the two of them in the limitless sky – so joyous, so carefree. She smiled, wishing this moment would last forever …

When the treatment ended, the leave-like sheet curled back automatically. Evelyn bounced out of the healing bed, feeling totally refreshed.

"Did you enjoy the acupressure treatment?" Guillermo asked her.

"It was great! Thanks for bringing me here," she answered brightly, smiling to herself as she recalled her incredible journey with Guillermo the Great White Eagle.

"Come, let's have lunch."

"No problem, I'd love to watch you eat," she said as cheerfully as she could manage.

"Why's that?" he asked, cocking an eyebrow. "Don't you want to try some Chinese food?"

"Of course I do!" said Evelyn eagerly. "It's just that I've never ever eaten real food, and I'm not sure this is a good time to start …" she faltered.

Guillermo laughed. "I'm sure this is a good time to try some food – trust me, I know a nice place in Chinatown perfect to start your first meal."

Guillermo took Evelyn to a majestic-looking Chinese tea house with red tiles and golden pillars. As they entered, they were greeted by a complex smell of Chinese tea, which Evelyn quite liked. She sniffed noisily and looked around: stored in glass jars, paper cartons and bamboo baskets were teas with fanciful names – Dragon Well Tea, Iron Goddess Tea, Silver Needle Tea …

The next room was a place of worship. There was a lingering smell of aromatic incense. Evelyn could see plenty of Chinese gods and goddesses in the glass cabinets along the wall. A whole roast pig lay on the table in the middle of the room, upon a flower bed, surrounded by smouldering incense sticks. Evelyn crouched over the table and saw that the pig had its eyes hollowed out, its mouth wide open. She shook her head. *How cruel.*

After that, they came to the main hall.

"A buffet!" Evelyn shouted excitedly.

Guillermo beamed at her. "An all-you-can-eat Chinese buffet – I thought you might like to try different kinds of food for your first meal."

Evelyn stood on tiptoe to see better: all over the hall, foods were placed on round tables that resembled little islands. There was the dumpling island with stacks of bamboo containers, the fried rice and noodles island with plenty of chopsticks standing ready, the roast meat island that looked barbaric, the seasonal fruit island that looked more suited for monkeys …

At that moment, Evelyn caught sight of a huge chocolate fountain in the far corner of the hall. Around the chocolate fountain were cakes, puddings, tarts and all things sweet! The temptation was too great to resist. Ignoring all the other choices in front of her, Evelyn dashed towards the dessert island and piled her plate with as much sweet food as it could carry.

When she got back, she found Guillermo seated at a table for two, already eating.

"What have you got there?" she asked spiritedly, pointing at

Guillermo's plate.

"I'm a vegetarian," explained Guillermo. "Let's see. I've got some sesame and mushroom noodles, a handful of tofu fried rice, several spinach and cheese dumplings, and some spicy spring rolls."

Evelyn looked back at her own plate: piled up like a mountain were mooncakes, fried ice-cream, egg custard tarts, coconut pudding, mango milk curd … it was embarrassing. All right, junk food probably would do her no harm. *But still …*

She gazed at Guillermo uncertainly. "I should probably get myself some rice and vegetables to go with my dessert –"

"Don't worry," Guillermo said quickly, "you can eat whatever you like in front of me. I don't mind at all."

Evelyn grinned and wasted no time in enjoying her dessert. It was her first time to eat – first bite, second bite, swallow – the food was heavenly, and she wanted more! She went on to wolf down everything on the plate like she hadn't eaten for a week.

Guillermo waited patiently while Evelyn finished her gigantic plate of dessert – the calories there could have fed at least four people. Between mouthfuls of cakes, Evelyn was in a very good mood.

"Guillermo, I have made up my mind. I'm going to China to learn kung fu! Will you teach me?" she said suddenly.

Guillermo narrowed his eyes. "If you want to be my student, you must be able to exercise self-control," he told her sternly.

"Oh," Evelyn muttered, feeling hurt. Tears began to well up in her eyes. "But you said I can eat whatever I like!" she shouted, pouting.

Guillermo shook his head. "I'm not talking about food. Of course I meant it when I said you can eat whatever you like."

He paused and frowned. "I'm talking about you falling on the cactuses. You were lucky this time, but you won't be lucky forever. If you don't exercise self-control, you will easily be killed in an accident or by Victor's robot army!"

Evelyn was dumbstruck for a moment. When she found her voice again, she said, "It won't happen again, I promise. I didn't mean to cause you all those troubles. I'm truly sorry."

"Self-discipline is especially important in kung fu," Guillermo added. "When you lack self-discipline, you're going to cause injuries to yourself or others even if you don't mean to!"

Evelyn nodded vigorously. "I fully understand, and I promise to exercise self-control and self-discipline. Now, can I be your student?"

Guillermo sighed, "In this case … yes."

Evelyn jumped up into the air as though she had just won the lottery. *Yay!*

Their rickshaw was waiting for them outside the Chinese tea house, beside the lotus pond. Evelyn could see bright red and orange koi fish swimming gracefully under the warm afternoon sun.

Guillermo looked at his watch.

"Today's the eighth of December, and the new term won't start until January. I'll give you a call around that time. For now, let me take you home –"

"I don't have a home," Evelyn said drily, "and if you mean Ronald's factory, I'm not going back."

"But the university's closed for the Christmas break. Where are you going to stay?"

"I'll find somewhere … anywhere but the factory!"

"Don't you need to pack for your journey?" Guillermo

suggested.

"No, I don't," she said without hesitation.

Guillermo was thoughtful for a moment.

"Evelyn, even if you have nothing to pack, I still think it's appropriate for you to go back and say goodbye."

"You don't understand – Ronald's going to kill me!" Evelyn shouted, running out of patience.

"He created you, that makes him your family –" Guillermo reasoned.

"You don't know Ronald at all!" Evelyn screamed in frustration. Then, remembering her promise to exercise self-control, she took a deep breath and continued, "Ronald's a robot killer, and he's going to kill me because I ran away from him."

"No, he won't," said Guillermo, striding purposefully to the rickshaw.

"What do you mean he won't?" Evelyn asked, catching up with Guillermo.

"I'm going to make a trip to Ronald's factory and tell him where you're going. It's customary: Master Chow knows Ronald. I can't just take you away," Guillermo said decisively.

"Sounds fair enough," Evelyn murmured.

"And you're coming with me."

Oh. Evelyn stared at him with a long face.

"Don't worry, Ronald won't dare to touch you in front of me," Guillermo added, brimming with confidence.

CHAPTER 6

Flying Supersonic

The beastly rickshaw took them out of Chinatown's red brick walls in no time. They changed to another car on the other side of the bridge – a glossy black race car. Although it was not armoured, its streamlined body reminded Evelyn of Ronald's car, which brought her to central London in the first place.

Guillermo opened the car door for her. Evelyn got in, thinking of Ronald … The race car engine roared like thunder, but Evelyn didn't care, her fear suddenly spiralling out of control.

"Don't make me go back," she wailed hysterically, "I don't want to be killed!"

Guillermo raised an eyebrow. "I thought we agreed you'll be safe, because you're with me," he said, giving her a quizzical look.

Evelyn continued wailing as though she didn't hear him, "However you put it – killed, terminated, reprogrammed – I'm going to die and you don't even care!" She burst into tears.

Guillermo patted her consolingly on the hand. "Nobody can harm you under my watch," he reassured her.

Evelyn stared fixedly at the stretch of highway ahead, her

cheeks tear-streaked.

"Are you going to message Ronald that we're visiting?" Guillermo asked after a while.

"No," Evelyn said tartly.

"All right, I'm going to message him for you."

He gave a nonchalant shrug and typed into the communication pad of the race car: "Good afternoon Ronald. This is Guillermo. I found Evelyn wandering the Cyber Hub while running errands for Master Chow, your old colleague. Evelyn's in my car now. We will arrive at around three."

Ronald's reply came promptly, "That's excellent news! I've been looking for Evelyn myself. Anything else I need to know?"

"Yes, Evelyn has something to tell you once she's back," Guillermo typed, glancing briefly in Evelyn's direction before pressing "send".

"Of course we can talk. She's most welcome," came Ronald's reply.

"That's it. See you soon." Guillermo ended the conversation and turned to Evelyn with a grin.

"So?"

"He, he's such a hypocrite!" Evelyn spluttered.

"We'll see," said Guillermo, sounding very non-committal.

They could see Stewart Corp's London factory even from afar. It stood out sharply in the horizon. Compared to the highway with plenty of trees planted on both sides, Ronald's factory looked rather barren with very little trees and the ground completely covered in concrete. There were lots of trucks and heavy vehicles standing idle outside the factory.

Their race car took them to the centre of the factory compound, until the main factory buildings stood right in front of their eyes: these were grand and modern, each at least 10-storey high, and with bridges around mid-level to connect them all. Despite the dust and sand from the highway, the external walls of the factory were all sparkling clean, with the company name TT Stewart Corporation firmly erected on the roof of the front building.

The apparent magnificence of the factory didn't fool Evelyn. *This is where it all began,* thought Evelyn, feeling shaken. Yesterday she left with Ronald in such haste she never got to look back; but now that she got a chance for a full view, Evelyn thought this place felt cold and oppressive. She felt almost ashamed to be created here. If the people working inside were as cold and oppressive …

"Do we really need to do this?" she asked Guillermo, her voice hoarse and pathetic.

"Come, Evelyn, everything's going to turn out fine." He held her hand tightly. "You can handle this. I will be by your side."

They walked up to the main gate. Guillermo led the way, with Evelyn following closely behind. Ronald was already waiting by the gate. Evelyn expected to see a raging Ronald, but was surprised to find him in a good mood.

"Hello, Evelyn!" Ronald called out warmly, welcoming her with open arms.

"Hi," she answered warily. *What's Ronald up to this time?*

"You must be Guillermo." Ronald held out his hand. "Thanks for bringing Evelyn back."

Guillermo returned the handshake. "It's nothing," he replied politely.

Ronald led Evelyn and Guillermo to a grand meeting room. In the middle of the room was a gemstone conference table, and around it were twelve creamy-white sofa armchairs. Ronald clicked a button behind the door: the high-tech white walls appeared to vanish, transforming magically into the panoramic view of a tropical grassland – Evelyn could see a herd of antelopes grazing on the meadows, and several giraffes reaching out to the tall trees with their long necks.

The rest of Ronald's team was there too: Bradley, John, Florence, Ethan and Suzanne. They were tasked with serving tea and snacks. Evelyn couldn't believe it – she was treated like a guest in this formidable factory.

After tea was served and everyone had settled down, Ronald breathed a sigh of relief, "So, we are finally back together." He eyed Evelyn with particular interest. "I'm glad you're not hurt."

Of course I was hurt, you have no idea, Evelyn grumbled in her heart.

"You know, you shouldn't have run off on your own," Ronald continued, frowning at her.

Evelyn wanted to scream: *This is so unfair!* Heaven knows she didn't just run away on her own. She had been dreading this moment of confrontation … but now, seeing that there were enough eyewitnesses around to stop Ronald killing her in a fit of rage, she was finally ready.

"Are you going to terminate me, or maybe reprogram me?" Evelyn asked in a shrill voice and started to shake. She was seething with rage; various other emotions flickered across her face – fear, insecurity, confusion …

Guillermo put a hand on her shoulder, which did little to calm her down. Ronald's team of scientists were staring at Evelyn open-mouthed, astounded by her reactions. Meanwhile, Ronald shifted in his seat. It was obvious that he too had not expected Evelyn's emotional outburst.

"Evelyn, I'm sorry if I gave you that impression," said Ronald after a minute. He looked up at the ceiling with a reminiscent expression. "Before you were created, I made sure your underlying computer program was healthy and virus-free. I vowed that once you were created, I'd treat you like a human, with dignity … to deal with all problems through conversation and teaching, but definitely not by reprogramming …"

"But you tried to activate my special firing system just before I ran for my life," Evelyn reminded him. "You clearly treated me like a robot!"

Ronald sighed and fixed his gaze on her. "You left me with no choice, Evelyn. Someone was clearly trying to hurt you, but you wouldn't even defend yourself. I had to protect you. It was my responsibility."

Evelyn glared at him. "You said you wanted me to be human, and yet, you created me to fight Victor. Aren't you –"

"Why not?" Ronald interrupted her, eager to explain. "You're a human with special talent. Your talent to fight Victor is a gift that you should never lay waste!"

Evelyn still didn't like Ronald, but at least she was convinced that he had no intention to kill her, and she found herself on speaking terms with him again.

"Ronald, there's something else we need to talk about," she began, glancing at Guillermo, who nodded encouragingly.

"Yes, Evelyn," said Ronald, a bit distractedly – he seemed to be still thinking about Victor.

"I've decided to learn kung fu in Master Chow's Yin-Yang Martial Arts University," Evelyn told him, clear and direct.

Ronald's shock at this bombshell news was visible: he froze in his armchair. Clearing his throat, he asked, "What good is learning kung fu?"

"Ask the headmaster –" Evelyn pointed at Guillermo quickly, evading the question.

Ronald shot Guillermo a dubious look. "You're the headmaster?"

"Yes, I am," Guillermo said confidently.

"Did you persuade Evelyn to learn kung fu?" Ronald interrogated Guillermo with barely concealed hostility.

"No, I didn't. She made her own choice," Guillermo answered, his tone calm and controlled.

"But you accepted her … into the kung fu university?" Ronald furrowed his brow.

"I accepted Evelyn as my student after she promised to exercise self-discipline and self-control," Guillermo replied in a cool-headed manner. "I believe Evelyn needs training in that area, especially if she is to defeat Victor one day …"

Ronald was rocking back and forth on his chair.

"When will you be back?" he asked Evelyn, curling his lips in displeasure.

"I'll return by summer," she answered, looking up to meet Ronald's eyes unflinchingly.

"I guess there's not much I can do to stop you then," he sighed with resignation. "I wish you good luck, Evelyn. See you again in summer."

Ronald escorted them out of the factory. As Evelyn climbed into the glossy black race car, she heard Ronald speaking to Guillermo, his voice uncharacteristically anxious: "You'll look after my girl, make sure she returns in one piece, won't you?"

To which Guillermo replied, his tone firm and serious, "I will."

They drove out of the factory compound and got back onto the highway. Evelyn put her head out of the car window and let out a wild whoop of joy – freedom was in the air! She peeked at Guillermo, daring him to lecture her about self-control. He didn't look bothered; he was even smiling slightly.

"Where are we going now?" asked Evelyn, her voice full of anticipation.

"Back to the hotel – I need to arrange our flight and do a bit of work before returning to the university," Guillermo told her, sounding almost apologetic. "Tonight, however, we can go to dinner together. They serve really good steaks at the hotel. I guess you've never tried steaks?"

"Steaks are great, but aren't you a vegetarian?" She was disappointed to hear that Guillermo would be busy this afternoon … but then, he wouldn't have become a headmaster at such a young age if he wasn't some kind of a workaholic.

"That's true, and they serve decent vegetarian dishes too," he said.

Back in the hotel suite, Guillermo sat at the mahogany desk and buried himself in his work. Soon it was dinner time and as promised, he took Evelyn down to the restaurant where she chose a rib-eye steak from the main course menu and four scoops of ice cream for dessert. The ice cream, in particular, put Evelyn in a very good mood.

"How long will the flight be?" she asked excitedly.

"Two hours and fifteen minutes."

"Just two hours and fifteen minutes?" Evelyn exclaimed, totally thrilled. "I thought China's halfway across the globe from London!"

"We'll be taking a supersonic plane," said Guillermo expertly. "Also known as the rocket plane, it's the fastest way to get us back to China."

"Wow, you must know a lot about flying," Evelyn cried out, impressed.

"I have to. I travel a lot." He grinned at her.

After dinner, they went to the airfield. A supersonic plane stood magnificently on the tarmac. It looked gorgeous under the gleaming beacons and spotlights in the airfield: the plane's body was bright scarlet, and its tail part was sparkling gold. Evelyn could see plenty of engines pointing in different directions – all rumbling powerfully, ready to go. The plane was, however, much smaller than what she expected.

"How many people will it carry?" she asked.

"Up to eight," Guillermo answered, "but this time, I've chartered the supersonic plane for our journey – so just the two of us."

"Just the two of us," Evelyn repeated, temporarily enchanted by the idea.

Guillermo led Evelyn up to the cockpit, where there were two front seats. He pointed her to the right. Evelyn touched the leather seat in wonder: *Wow,* it was luxuriously soft, with plenty of cushioning for shock absorption.

"Buckle up your seat belt. We'll be taking off shortly," Guillermo urged her. "This plane goes up like a rocket. You don't want to be banging your head against the roof."

He made sure Evelyn was secured in her seat, and then asked, "Are you ready?"

"Yes, I am. Let's fly!" Evelyn shouted, wide-eyed.

At first, their plane climbed up at an angle, gradually putting London behind them. A screen in front showed them their real-time altitude: 1 km … 5.5 km … 10 km.

As they reached 10 km in height, the plane pointed its nose upward and shot up vertically, like a rocket. Beyond the windscreen, stars were twinkling in the night sky. Evelyn looked sideways and saw that she was lying side by side with Guillermo – both stuck to their seats with their knees bent. Their altitude was rising quickly: 10 km … 20 km … 30 km.

At 30 km high, their plane stopped rocketing up. The sounds from the engines were now different, and the plane automatically got back to the horizontal position.

Guillermo smiled at Evelyn. "How was your first rocket plane experience?"

"Fantastic. What a ride!" she gasped, much impressed.

Their plane was now travelling forward at supersonic speed. Evelyn leaned towards the cockpit windscreen until her field of vision was completely filled by the transcendent beauty outside: she could see countless stars twinkling upon an infinitely deep and mysterious universe. The world outside seemed totally free, boundlessly wild …

Evelyn let her imagination take flight: she imagined just the two of them soaring at 30 km high, with arms as wings, in this otherworldly atmosphere …

"Bravo!" she yelled.

"What?" Guillermo asked.

Evelyn stared at him with trance-like eyes. "Wouldn't it be wonderful if we could just open the door and fly outside – free as a bird!" she said wildly.

"Don't, you'll kill us both!" He reacted tensely, and managed to relax only after he was certain Evelyn was joking. Looking amused now, Guillermo added slowly, "If you fancy flying like a bird, there are actually ways to do so. One day, Evelyn, I can teach you."

Towards the end of their flight, the sun began to rise: above them, the infinitely deep and mysterious universe remained unchanged; below them, the sky turned from deep dark to orange to bright blue. The universe and sky joined together at the horizon, forming an infinitely wide world …

Evelyn was drifting off into reveries when Guillermo said, "We'll land soon." He was regarding her fondly. "We can land with minimal turbulence, or we can do it in an aerobatic-inspired way. Which would you prefer?"

Evelyn's eyes lit up. "Definitely the aerobatics – something not for the faint-hearted!"

"All right. Are you buckled up safely?"

"Yes, I am," Evelyn shouted, pulling on her seat belt to show how tight it was.

"In that case …" Guillermo trailed off. He typed in a few commands on the control screen.

Immediately afterwards, their rocket plane pointed its nose upward. It went eerie silent, before free-falling through the sky.

"Whoa!" Evelyn let out a yell of exhilaration.

At 10 km high, the plane stopped falling with a mighty upward jerk. Just as Evelyn thought the excitement was over, more was yet to come! Their rocket plane started to spin and roll out of the sky, dropping to 8 km … 6 km … sometimes nosediving, sometimes flipping on its back, sometimes rotating like a disk … until at 1 km high, it finally stabilised, flying straight again.

Evelyn looked out of the cockpit windscreen and found herself above large expanse of nature. Billows of clouds swirled around the mountain tops. Under a thin layer of snow, there were all shades of green: yellowish green, pastel green, bright green, dark green …

“Where are we?” she asked Guillermo, gaping at the exotic world beneath them.

“Sichuan, above the nature reserve,” he answered warmly. “Do you like it?”

“The scenery’s breathtaking.” She was in awe. “And where is the university?” She scanned the landscape for school buildings, sports grounds, and halls of residence.

“Over there,” said Guillermo, pointing to their left, “behind that thick forest.”

As their plane made a sharp turn before landing, Evelyn caught a brief, fleeting glimpse of the university.

The supersonic plane landed smoothly on a small airfield in Sichuan’s nature reserve. Guillermo swiftly unbuckled both of their seat belts.

“Come.” He offered his hand to help Evelyn out of the cockpit.

It was a sunny morning in Sichuan. Stepping out onto the airfield, Evelyn could feel the cold air and fresh breeze brushing against her face. Guillermo turned to her.

“It’s a twenty-minute walk from here to campus, and the scenery along the way is beautiful,” said Guillermo.

“I’d love to see the scenery,” Evelyn exclaimed, stretching out her muscles after the flight. “It’d be nice to walk in this lovely weather.”

The two of them walked briskly up the mountain. Five minutes later, they arrived at “China Conservation and Research Centre for the Giant Pandas”. Evelyn could see pandas sleeping on trees and eating bamboo leaves on the hill, looking absolutely cuddly in their black and white fur. The research centre was a cutting-edge, two-storey construction with all kinds of animal-monitoring technologies set up on the rooftop. Rustic-looking wood and stone huts were erected in the surrounding area.

Further uphill, they came upon a sign with an arrow pointing to "Yin-Yang Martial Arts University". Evelyn glanced around, but there was no building in sight … just trees, and a forest.

"This is the University's outer zone," Guillermo explained, "where we grow food based on the permaculture design."

Almost immediately, they were greeted by a handwritten sign that read "Edible Forest". Cheerful images of candy trees popped up in Evelyn's mind. To her disappointment, she found herself looking at crooked old trees and wild thorny weeds – supposedly edible. *Yuck!*

They also passed several huge glass greenhouses, as well as fields with rows and rows of colourful vegetables. The Sichuanese Garden was particularly pleasing to the eyes, with its Chinese pavilions and lively fish ponds.

The last stretch of path had tall trees towering on both sides. After that, they arrived at the main campus.

CHAPTER 7

Panda, Monkey, and Fox-Leopard

The campus was very quiet as most students and staff had gone home for the Christmas break. Evelyn and Guillermo ran up some stairs, turned a corner, and entered a building.

"Welcome," said Guillermo, "to Student Lodge, where you'll be staying for this term."

Student Lodge was an eco-friendly building. Evelyn could see solar panels installed all over the roof. Trees were planted around the building to provide shades. Inside, the windows were specially positioned to let in sunlight.

"Here are the details of your room." He handed her a sheet containing her room number and key code.

Evelyn instantly memorised the entire sheet. "Thank you," she murmured.

"Now, let's talk about what you may do during Christmas," Guillermo continued. "I've got some good suggestions for you." He smiled at her.

Evelyn looked up. "Great! I'm listening."

"As our school is right next to the nature reserve, most students do volunteer work there. You can volunteer to take care of the Chinese giant pandas, for example. Most people love that."

For a moment, Evelyn didn't know what to say. She had come to China to learn martial arts ... and now, she was offered this once-in-a-lifetime opportunity to get close to the famous pandas too. *What's not to like?*

"Yes! I'm definitely going to do the panda volunteering," she answered passionately. "What other animals can I volunteer to take care of? Any endangered species that need a helping hand, or rescued animals that need to be nursed back to health?"

Guillermo gazed at her fondly.

"Evelyn, I'm glad you like animals. Let's go to see Director Zhang at the nature reserve. He's responsible for student volunteers, and has a knack for matching students with animals."

Evelyn followed Guillermo to the nature reserve's visitor centre: the state-of-the-art glass building was filled with control panels, lots of interactive screens, and hologram projections of animals that lived there. Director Zhang's office was at the far end of the second level. As they entered his office, Evelyn noticed Zhang had very rough skin, was dressed in a tailored suit, and wore a gold wristwatch. At first, Guillermo chatted with Zhang in Chinese. He then switched to English to tell Zhang about Evelyn's passion for all kinds of animals – pandas, endangered species, rescued animals ...

Director Zhang rubbed his chin with his stubby fingers, his expression thoughtful. He spoke to Evelyn directly, "The headmaster tells me you have a big heart, and he's rarely mistaken. Let me see ... You may take care of a panda from our nursery – everybody likes pandas. I've also got a golden snub-nosed monkey – an endangered species – that needs to be cared for. And if you're feeling brave, why not consider caring for the fox-leopard? He's the product of an unsuccessful biological engineering experiment, so be warned: he's extremely vicious!"

"No problem," Evelyn replied gallantly. "I'll take care of all three of them."

Director Zhang peered at Evelyn from behind his wrinkled eyelids. "The panda's friendly, but the monkey had been bullied so he will bite you. Needless to say, the fox-leopard is the most dangerous. Your job is to feed these three animals daily and –"

He scribbled a website on a piece of paper and shoved it into Evelyn's hand. "Here, you'll find all about volunteering in the nature reserve – there's a video prepared by our team of Chinese researchers and experts. Volunteering here doesn't require professional knowledge, but it does require much heart and time." He pointed at Evelyn's chest good-naturedly. "Remember to put on the special alloy suit when working in the enclosures of the monkey and fox-leopard. You don't want to be killed by either of them!"

Before they left, Guillermo cracked a Chinese joke with Director Zhang. Evelyn watched on as the two men laughed heartily.

As soon as they were out of the visitor centre, Evelyn exclaimed with admiration, "Guillermo, this is the first time I hear you speak Chinese, and you are so fluent!"

"Thanks for the compliment," he answered modestly. "Took me quite some time to learn to be honest – Chinese jokes, proverbs, folklores …"

"I heard that Chinese is extremely difficult to learn," Evelyn blurted out.

"Yes … especially for unenhanced humans like myself," he said with humour.

They walked back to Student Lodge together.

"This is where I leave you. If you need to find me, I'll be in Headmaster Mansion."

"Good, see you soon!" Evelyn waved goodbye cheerfully, but Guillermo suddenly remembered something.

He reached out and gave Evelyn's hand a squeeze. "Be careful around the biting monkey and the biologically-engineered fox-leopard –"

"Don't worry about me. I can take care of myself," she said, surprised by the concern in Guillermo's voice.

"Evelyn, if you unfortunately injure yourself, let me know immediately. Understand?" It sounded almost like an order, and his eyes were blazing.

"All right." Evelyn nodded, feeling overwhelmed by his protectiveness.

Guillermo sighed and let go of Evelyn's hand. "See you soon then."

Over the next two weeks, Evelyn divided her time between the three animals. Life in the nature reserve must have been good to the animals, because they were all very alert and energetic.

Naturally, Evelyn loved her panda the most: the one-year-old girl was a fluffy ball of black and white, about half the size of an adult panda. She lived in the high-tech panda nursery, where Evelyn could see robots cleaning the floors and changing the straw bedding – *No wonder everything is so clean and tidy!* Evelyn was tasked with feeding the panda, measuring her furs and paws, and playing games … The cute little panda followed Evelyn everywhere around the nursery; she didn't like cuddles, but loved to be scratched behind her ears.

The golden snub-nosed monkey, meanwhile, had a totally different personality. Despite looking rather handsome with a distinctive blue face and short golden hair, he was always nervous. Every time Evelyn put on the special alloy suit and got into his forest-like enclosure to feed him, he would climb down the trees nervously, clawing and biting at the branches along the way. He also had this nasty habit of biting Evelyn after a few mouthfuls, which really tried Evelyn's patience.

The fox-leopard was even worse. Living alone in a savanna-like enclosure with plenty of grass and rocks, he was as cunning as a fox, and as aggressive as a leopard. He would attack Evelyn's arms and legs, biting into her alloy suit, as soon as she set foot in his enclosure; on a really bad day, he would even jump up to snap at her head and neck.

On Christmas Eve, Evelyn received a message from Guillermo, inviting her for dinner at Headmaster Mansion the following day. Feeling a leap of excitement, she replied quickly, "Yes, I'll be coming!" She then set off to the nature reserve in a buoyant mood.

On Christmas Day, Evelyn went to Headmaster Mansion at sunset. Standing on a small hill and silhouetted against the orange sky was a two-storey house in traditional Chinese style. There were two stone lions guarding the front door, and dozens of red lanterns hanging outside. Evelyn walked up to the front door, wanted to find the door bell, but instead noticed a brass knocker in the shape of a Chinese lion's head. Amused, she hit the front door three times with it.

Guillermo came out wearing a green Christmas jumper with an enormous Santa Claus on it – the beard of Santa was 3D and looked like the strings of a mop.

"Come in, Evelyn, welcome to my house," he greeted her warmly.

"Merry Christmas, Guillermo," Evelyn answered joyfully, almost laughing out loud at his funny jumper.

The front room of Headmaster Mansion was very official-looking. Evelyn could see Chinese calligraphy, paintings and scrolls on the walls. At the centre of the room was a large solid wood conference table, and on the table were six very eye-catching porcelain figurines –

"Chinese dragons!" Evelyn exclaimed, amazed. The porcelain dragons were in red, orange, blue, green, white and black.

"I bought them from six different Chinese provinces during my travels," Guillermo explained, looking proud of himself. "It's an on-going project of mine: if I find something nice, I'm going to add to my collection."

The living room was equally amazing. Evelyn was dumbstruck by the amount of medals, trophies and certificates displayed on the walls and in glass cupboards.

"Are these all yours?" she asked Guillermo.

"Yes." His voice was casual. "They form a small part of what I won over the years: I only display awards from major competitions, and the rest, I keep in the basement."

"What's this?" Evelyn asked curiously, pointing at a gold medal that Guillermo won some twenty years ago.

Guillermo came closer. "That's the Martial Arts Youth Championship, my first international competition," he said, his expression reminiscent. "I competed as an underage athlete … I was eight, and the eldest kid was thirteen … it was hard, but I won."

"What a child prodigy!" Evelyn praised wholeheartedly.

Guillermo smiled. "Come, you must be starving. I've prepared lots of food for you."

He led Evelyn into the dining room.

"Wow!" Evelyn cried out when she saw the heaps of food covering the dining table. Guillermo had prepared a feast of western desserts – there were plenty of blueberries, strawberries and raspberries on top of the cakes – even the air smelt sweet. Looking around, Evelyn could see that the dining room had been decorated with Christmas trees, twinkle lights, wrapped presents and greeting cards. It was the kind of atmosphere you would create for a traditional Christmas dinner with family and friends.

"How many guests have you invited?"

Guillermo chuckled. "Just one – you. Don't be fooled by the amount of food; my guest has a big appetite, and I need to make sure she has enough to eat!"

"Did you make all these yourself?" asked Evelyn, salivating at the irresistible desserts.

"You can say that." He pointed at the high-tech appliances in his kitchen. "The baking's done by the smart oven, and the ingredients are Christmas gifts from my family in Europe – blessings from my family, because you can't find these ingredients in China."

"Will your family miss you … not being home on Christmas Day?" Evelyn asked.

"Um, they should be fine for a while. I've just visited them on my last trip to London."

"So you are from London?" she pursued.

"I grew up in a leafy village in Kent, but I was born in London."

"Same as me. I was born in London too!" she chimed in brightly. They burst out laughing.

After dinner, they sat on the sofa. Evelyn found herself facing a wall shelf full of robot action figures. She smiled to herself: *Guillermo's still a child at heart.*

There was a robot domestic helper cleaning up the dining table: the robot was taller than a man, probably twice as wide, and was fully coated in shiny metal plates like one of those "Transformers" from comic books.

"I have never seen a robot domestic helper quite as marvellous-looking as yours!" said Evelyn, impressed.

"That's because I designed and built that robot from scratch," Guillermo answered with a bit of pride. Turning serious, he said, "Evelyn, the induction camp for new students starts on January the second. You want to be in tip-top form for that."

"Why? What happens in the induction camp?" she asked, sensing something important here.

"Your mental qualities will be tested," Guillermo answered mysteriously.

"My mental qualities?" Evelyn muttered. "What happens if I fail?"

"We don't fail anyone: students give up on their own. Those who give up pack their bags and go home."

"What!" Evelyn was shocked.

Guillermo placed a hand on her shoulder and gazed into her eyes confidently. "Evelyn, all you need to remember is: Never give up! There's not much else you can do to prepare for the challenge, so just relax and focus on your voluntary work for now."

On the night before the induction camp, Student Lodge was filled with laughter. Students had returned from their Christmas break. They were chatting loudly in the corridor, looking forward to the new school term. Meanwhile, Evelyn paced her room restlessly. She was probably the only one in the entire building who needed to face the notorious induction camp, as the new students would all be arriving the next day.

Evelyn usually stayed in her room after dark, but on this night, feeling particularly lonely and nervous, she remembered her animal friends. For once, Evelyn felt the need to go for a night walk, just to say goodnight to them.

Jogging into the nature reserve, Evelyn's first stop was the panda nursery. Her panda girl was asleep, but awoke when she sensed Evelyn, and came down the hill to let Evelyn scratch behind her ears. Evelyn then went to visit the golden snub-nosed monkey, who briefly opened his sleepy eyes to glance at her.

Lastly, Evelyn went to visit the fox-leopard. Even from afar, Evelyn could see his two evil eyes gleaming in the darkness – he seemed to be lying in wait for his prey. Evelyn approached his enclosure cautiously. She was going to say goodnight from the outside, when without warning, the fox-leopard leapt through the air, his paws outstretched, as though he wanted to maul her to death!

The fox-leopard's hunting instinct took Evelyn by surprise. In the face of imminent death, her body went into automatic mode. She threw herself backwards with terrifying force, landing at the base of the opposite enclosure – a base made of sharp jagged rocks for a desert-like habitat. *AAARGH!*

The stabbing pain in Evelyn's head and back made her want to scream at the top of her lungs, but she clenched her teeth … *No, I mustn't scream, not unless I want to wake the entire nature reserve up!* Evelyn touched her head and felt several big wet gashes. Using her infrared vision, she saw her own blood dripping onto the rocks. A chill ran down Evelyn's spine: she looked at the fox-leopard, expecting him to go berserk, knowing only too well how the beast craved bloody meat. To Evelyn's amazement, the fox-leopard simply walked away.

Enduring the stabbing pain, Evelyn tried to stop the bleeding by pressing on her wounds. It wasn't too effective, as some of the injuries reached all the way down to her metal core. Evelyn decided to find Guillermo: humiliating though it was to have to visit him when she was covered in blood, she needed someone to stitch up her wounds.

Evelyn went to Headmaster Mansion and knocked on its grand door. Guillermo came out, wearing a blue dressing gown. Evelyn thought his face paled at the sight of her, but it was hard to tell under the lantern light.

"Please come in," he said, pushing the door wide open.

Out of the corner of her eye, Evelyn caught Guillermo frowning to himself. Suddenly, she was overcome by the feeling that she must make everything clear. She had to tell him it was not her fault.

Evelyn paused beside the large conference table – upon which the six porcelain dragons sat elegantly – and began to explain herself: "I have been careful … I was outside the enclosure … The fox-leopard …"

"Did you lose a lot of blood?" Guillermo interrupted her anxiously.

"I guess not," she answered uncertainly.

He gently pushed Evelyn forward and led her towards a chair. "You need to rest," he said firmly. "Stay right there. I'll be back in a moment."

Guillermo returned with a tray of medical equipment.

"I'm sorry to bother you," said Evelyn apologetically. "I just need you to patch me up, then I'll leave, and you can go back to sleep."

Guillermo quickly cleaned up her wounds with his huge but gentle hands.

"Evelyn, I meant it when I said you should let me know if you injure yourself. You did right coming to me tonight."

For a moment, Evelyn was lost for words. Then she said in a small voice, "I was worried you'd lecture me about self-control, self-discipline, and all those things."

Guillermo shrugged. "I have no intention to do that, though I'm glad you still remember your promises. Accidents do sometimes happen when caring for difficult animals, no matter how careful you are."

Evelyn breathed a sigh of relief. "I thought you would tell me not to set foot in the nature reserve ever again, for my own safety!"

Guillermo shook his head. "Quite the contrary, Evelyn, I want you to carry on. You are kind and compassionate, and I think you've been doing a great job caring for those animals."

"Oh," Evelyn uttered. This was unexpected.

"Director Zhang has a high opinion of you," Guillermo added, his tone calm and reassuring.

"Really? I rarely see him around," said Evelyn, surprised.

"He doesn't need to. He has surveillance cameras installed all over the nature reserve," Guillermo told her. "Zhang thanked me for finally sending a student who really knows how to communicate with animals."

"How come?" cried Evelyn. "Don't most students have cats and dogs at home?"

"That's exactly the problem. Zhang complains to me that

most students treat wild animals like pets," Guillermo said drily.

"What a pity," Evelyn chortled.

It took more than an hour for Guillermo to stitch up all of Evelyn's wounds. Afterwards, he escorted her back to Student Lodge, stopping outside the front porch.

It was a starry night. He patted her on the shoulder. "Happy new year, Evelyn, and good luck with the induction camp tomorrow."

CHAPTER 8

The Horror Cave

The first part of the induction camp was held in a man-made cave in the mountain. Evelyn set out thirty minutes before her assigned time. Walking up a flight of spiral stone steps with strangely shaped rocks along the way, she arrived at a large cave chamber with a high domed ceiling, thick round columns, and walls which were polished to near-perfect smoothness. Evelyn could see colourful lights shining around – orange, green, blue – the dancing lights gave this spacious cave a very mysterious feeling.

Standing at the centre of the cave was a stern-looking kung fu master. He was tall, lean, and dressed in a black robe. Three students had gathered around him – all male, all strong and muscular. Evelyn walked towards the group, feeling nervous. A sickening thought struck her: *Are we going to fight each other?*

The kung fu master spoke in a deep, booming voice. "Welcome to Yin-Yang Martial Arts University. I am Master Lin. The induction camp is mandatory for all new students. Each year, the challenge is different. This year, it is the Horror Cave. Your task is to collect the five glowing stones in your assigned cave and come out alive."

Evelyn's stomach churned: she wondered what horrors lay

inside those caves.

"You'll be given a device with two buttons. The first is the emergency button. You may use it to alert our medical team. Our doctors will also be monitoring your vital signs –"

"Oh!" Evelyn cried out jumpily. She quickly apologised for interrupting, but the damage had been done. When Master Lin spoke again, he was staring at Evelyn directly, as though addressing her alone.

"The second is the give-up button. Don't press it unless you're absolutely sure. Giving up on your own is the only way to fail the induction challenge – you will be asked to pack up and leave."

Afterwards, they waited for their names to be called. Evelyn sat on a rock anxiously. She glanced around and found to her consolation that her muscular schoolmates were as anxious as herself. One of them was pacing up and down restlessly. Another was facing the cave wall muttering his prayers. The third one was warming himself up so furiously you would think he was about to fight a lion.

From where they were waiting, Evelyn could see four separate caves pointing in different directions. She craned her neck to get a better view, but there was not much to see as the entrances were each blocked up by a heavy wooden door. At that moment, Evelyn heard ear-piercing screams coming from the cave behind her, followed by an ominous silence.

"Evelyn Smith!" the announcer called out all of a sudden.

Evelyn jumped to her feet. A 3D projection of an arrow directed her to the cave on her right.

Stepping into her assigned cave, Evelyn felt like she had entered another world: this was a high-tech simulation of a tropical rainforest. She found herself standing on wet mud, under canopies of trees. She could hear birds chirping and an eagle flapping its wings. The monkeys were crying wildly, and so were the frogs.

The simulated rainforest seemed to go on endlessly. It was beautiful in a disorientating way. Evelyn couldn't see the cave boundaries. She wondered whether all caves featured the same landscape? Temporarily mesmerised, it took Evelyn some time to remember what this place really was – the Horror Cave, and she was here to face some unknown horrors!

As if on cue, the whole landscape, bursting with life since she stepped in, suddenly turned eerie silent. A chill ran down Evelyn's spine. *Where have all the wildlife gone?*

Evelyn then heard the sound of many legs. Filled with trepidation, she looked down to see two slimy giant centipedes crawling around her feet. In the blink of an eye, they had made their way up her shoes and were about to get under her trousers. Evelyn's eyes widened in shock when she spotted their horrendous stingers and pincers –

"Noooo!" she screamed hysterically. She needed to get those devilish centipedes off her legs. *Now!*

But before she even had time to start getting rid of the centipedes, Evelyn felt something hairy moving on her head. Next second, long, oily, jointed spider legs appeared in front of her eyes. She froze: it was a black widow spider. The venomous creature was crawling all over her face, making its way from her head to her neck. It had reached her shirt, and was putting its disgusting legs under her clothes as if tucking itself under a comfortable blanket …

The full scale of the present horror hit home: Evelyn was alone, surrounded by real, venomous insects! She wanted to press the give-up button, but forced herself to stay calm: *These insects are not computer simulated … they bite … they're going to kill me if I don't get rid of them.* It was now or never.

"Do it!" Evelyn ordered herself.

Screaming at the top of her lungs, Evelyn lashed out at the venomous insects with all her might! It was mad and instinctive. She just kept on hitting them, persevering, not stopping till she had killed every one of her enemies.

When she was done, Evelyn stood on the dead bodies of the black widow spider and centipedes, feeling dazed. There was a dull ache all over her body. She refused to believe that she had been bitten. *I must have strained my muscles,* she tried to convince herself. In the back of her mind, Master Lin's words came rushing back: "Your task is to collect the five glowing stones … and come out alive."

Something was glowing on the dry leaves about twenty steps ahead: the first stone! The problem was, several large scorpions were circling round the stone.

Gingerly, Evelyn tiptoed to the stone, taking extra care not to stamp on the scorpions – but the scorpions were brutal. Evelyn yelped in pain as they bit her on the left ankle. Hopping on her right foot, she grabbed the first stone, then limped away hastily to find a protruding tree root to rest on. She held up her left foot to see how bad the bite was: there were two red marks, both swelling to the size of peas before her eyes.

Nursing her injured foot, Evelyn despaired. *What good is being careful when I'm going to be bitten anyway?*

Throwing caution to the wind, Evelyn leapt towards the second stone – it was sitting on a tree branch, next to some giant tarantulas. She went on to dig out the third glowing stone, which was buried in sand, under a scorpion-infested mound.

The fourth stone lay at the bottom of a pond. Evelyn could see it glowing in the water. To get to the pond, she must cross some semi-submerged rocks with centipedes on them … Evelyn let out a howl of anguish, and waded through the shallow water as fast as she could. When she returned with the stone, she found half a dozen centipedes clinging onto her trousers. She screamed, then shook her legs like crazy. After what seemed an eternity, the centipedes all let go of her.

Evelyn realised the aches in her body were sharpening and getting worse. She didn't bother to check where she was bitten this time. *I'm still standing,* she told herself, and tried not to think any further.

The last stone was glowing inside a treasure box, the style commonly used by pirates. The box was opened, with treasures spilt out. Evelyn could see spiders and scorpions all over the box – there were so many of them they were climbing on top of each other in layers. As if that wasn't enough, centipedes were patrolling the moist sand around the box like soldiers …

This was beyond horrible: it was nightmarish. Evelyn's legs felt like jelly. She was seriously tempted to press the give-up button, but refrained. *I have come so far, what could possibly be worse than being sent back to Ronald's factory?* She steadied herself and briefly considered various strategies of getting the venomous insects out of the way – probing, hitting, distracting – it seemed that whichever method she chose, she would still be bitten to death.

"So be it!" Evelyn said aloud, steeling herself for the final blow.

She took a deep breath, then quickly stepped over the patrolling centipedes, diving her hand through the spiders and scorpions into the treasure box. For a moment, so many teeth, pincers and stingers attacked her all at once that she had to withdraw her hand.

"AAAAAAARGH!" Evelyn screamed and jumped back. Enduring the avalanche of pain as venom poured into her body, she tried again. She could see the last glowing stone sitting tantalisingly in the treasure box, but her hands were shaking violently because of the venom, and her legs were giving way. It was with great effort that Evelyn managed to touch the fifth glowing stone …

Mercifully, the exit door opened as she touched the stone. In the glare of the sun, the dreadful insects instantly let go of her and scattered back to the dark cave. Evelyn gasped for air: she never knew fresh air tasted so heavenly. Temporarily refreshed, Evelyn picked up the fifth glowing stone and wobbled out of the cave. She felt so proud of herself: *I did it, I did it!*

The next thing Evelyn knew, she had lost her footing and was falling. She tried to break the fall with both hands, but her body simply wouldn't respond. She panicked. The ground was rushing up to meet her face, and there was nothing she could do about it – she was going to hit her head.

To Evelyn's surprise, Guillermo suddenly appeared by her side. With incredible agility, he placed one hand against her back, another behind her head, before lowering her to the ground like a delicate vase.

He squatted down beside her and took out a stainless steel flask. "Drink this," he murmured, holding Evelyn's head patiently while she swallowed. It was a curious concoction, the luxurious sweetness of milk chocolate masking the bitter taste of herbal medicine. Then, darkness closed in.

Light filled the room. Evelyn stretched out on her bed in Student Lodge and opened her eyes. She felt stiff. She sat up, yawned and stared out of the window – it was bright outside. *How long have I been asleep*? She checked the time, and was startled: two days! It was already the fourth of January. Evelyn had missed the entire induction camp apart from the Horror Cave … which was a pity … as she had been hoping to make a few friends during the ice-breaking part of the camp …

Never mind that, thought Evelyn, shaking her head with dismay. At least she got up in time for the start-of-term ceremony for new students, to be held in the Great Hall that evening. Really, things could have been far worse.

Evelyn combed her hair, got dressed, and at four thirty, left Student Lodge ready to meet her schoolmates.

The Great Hall of Yin-Yang Martial Arts University was an eye-catching traditional construction which could be seen even from afar. It was three-storey high, covered with red tiles, and very majestic-looking. Getting closer, Evelyn noticed the eaves on each level were elaborately decorated, with stone animals standing on significant feng shui spots. As she prepared to enter, she was amazed by the Chinese scriptures and calligraphy on the walls. It struck her that this must be a very cultured and scholarly place. Evelyn pushed open the door gently, careful not to disturb the peace and quietness inside …

What a shock! Far from being a place for quiet study, this was clearly a place to prepare for battles. Evelyn looked up and saw long tridents and giant axes dangling from the beams, pointing to her head. Around her, swords and daggers were lodged into the walls with their sharp ends pointing out intimidatingly. There were also iron whips, crossbows and huge sickles hanging on the walls. Evelyn gave herself a moment to take in the scene, and then walked towards the dining tables.

Fifteen round tables had been set up, and at least thirty students had arrived. Evelyn quickly looked up at the teacher's table on stage. There Guillermo was, presiding over the hall as headmaster. He was talking to a white-haired man beside him – that must be Master Chow, the school founder. Also sitting on stage was Master Lin, whom Evelyn recognised from the induction camp, and Director Zhang from the nature reserve. There were another four men and three women who must be teachers too. Guillermo caught Evelyn's eyes and gave her a wide grin. She grinned back.

Evelyn was trying to find a seat, preferably among a group of girls, when someone standing beside her suddenly shouted in a loud, shrill voice, making her jump.

"Here she comes, the idiot who was stung a thousand times in the Horror Cave and came out looking like a pig!"

Evelyn quickly turned to the voice and found a finger with red polished nail pointing rudely at her nose. The owner of both the voice and the finger was a tall, arrogant-looking girl with waist-length blonde hair. She was flanked by two muscular boys who were howling with laughter at her joke. For a moment, Evelyn felt so angry she wanted to punch that girl in the face: *How dare you make fun of me!* Then she remembered her promise to Guillermo: self-discipline and self-control … With much effort, she reined in her temper and walked away. She could now hear that hateful girl boasting loudly about how she took all five glowing stones and got out of the cave in record-breaking time, without being stung by a single insect, thanks to her nanotech, full-body raincoat …

Evelyn eventually found a place among four pale-skinned, dark-haired girls. She thought they already knew each other, and was surprised to learn that they actually came from different countries and had only just met – Heewon was from Korea, Momoko was from Japan, Lily was a Chinese American, and Xiaojin came from Canton China. The conversation went well until they moved on to talk about their families. While Momoko was describing animatedly her skiing trip on Mount Fuji during Christmas, Evelyn faced a new problem: she had no family, and she sensed that these girls were not ready to make friend with someone born in a factory.

Luckily, the ceremony began just in time. Master Chow and Guillermo got to their feet and welcomed everyone to the school. Master Chow announced that six students gave up in the Horror Cave – "they were in good health, but of course asked to leave" – which meant there were seventy-two new students this year. He and Guillermo then walked to the entrance of the Great Hall, where there was a large bronze bell similar to the type used in Buddhist temples to summon monks. Master Chow held a large hammer to strike the bell from the outside: once … twice … thrice …

After each strike, there was a clear bell sound, followed by rumbling reverberation. No one spoke as the Great Hall was filled with the solemn tones. When the last reverberation died away, Master Chow announced cheerfully: "Let the feast begin!"

It was a buffet-style dinner. There was the induction camp special (deep fried spider, scorpion and centipede), several Sichuanese hot pots (filled with beef, pork, duck, eggplant and seasonal greens), and various Chinese dishes (fried rice, chow mein, dumplings and spring rolls to name a few). Evelyn was impressed, but when it came to putting food into her mouth, she had only one thing in mind – the sweet and comforting! She glanced towards the dessert aisle and noticed there was no one there, whereas the other aisles were bustling with students. Evelyn wondered briefly whether it would look odd to be the only person starting dinner with dessert? Presently, she decided: *No, I can't care too much.* She needed to please herself. Speaking of oddities, there were really far odder things about herself than her love of dessert.

Evelyn was dashing towards the dessert aisle, her mind filled with images of the sweet food she had tasted recently, when she had to stop abruptly. When did Guillermo get off the stage, Evelyn had no idea; but there he was, and he was not alone. Blocking Evelyn's way were Guillermo and Director Zhang – two big men, each with a wide smile. *Good heavens!* thought Evelyn. *What do they want from me?* Evelyn had never seen Director Zhang in such a good mood. She remembered that when she first set foot in the nature reserve, Zhang looked at her with a stern face and only laughed with Guillermo. This time it was different: Zhang's warmth extended to Evelyn too.

"Your animals are missing you," he said softly.

"Oh, I'm sorry," Evelyn answered, blushing. It had only been three days since she last visited them.

"Don't be sorry," said Zhang. "Just come back when you are well enough. Animals like those you are caring for … the unloved and the young ones … they are very loyal to the hands that give them food and kindness."

Zhang had barely finished his sentence when Master Chow came to join them. Guillermo stepped forward and introduced them to each other.

"Chow, this is Evelyn. Evelyn, this is Master Chow."

Evelyn immediately found herself under the shrewd, scrutinising gaze of Master Chow. After a few unnerving seconds, Chow softened his gaze.

"Nice to finally meet you, Evelyn. Heard a lot about you from Guillermo."

Evelyn glanced at Guillermo, but his face revealed nothing.

Master Chow then put a hand on Evelyn's shoulder – a warm and powerful hand – warmth instantly spread through Evelyn's skin and flesh towards her metal core.

"Eat well," he told her, before walking away with Guillermo and Director Zhang.

A group of students had now gathered around the school founder and headmaster, eager to chat about kung fu. Evelyn smiled to herself, feeling elated. Guillermo had made her day by coming to her first before speaking to other students. It was a small act, but meant a lot to Evelyn … so much so that she no longer needed to seek comfort from sweet desserts. She actually wanted to eat like a normal person tonight, which was unprecedented.

When Evelyn got back to her table, the girls asked her about London. Smiling radiantly, Evelyn shared with them all the interesting facts about Chinatown and Cyber Hub. She also promised to take them around London next time they came to visit.

As the feast drew to a close, Master Chow and Guillermo walked to the entrance. Hammering the bronze bell once to draw everyone's attention, they led the way out of the Great Hall into the open air. Master Chow then declared in a booming voice, "For good luck, and as tradition goes –"

Firecrackers exploded around them deafeningly; fireworks

were propelled into the sky, turning the dark night into myriads of sparkling colours. Immersed in the joyous atmosphere, students started humming, singing, holding hands and hugging each other. But for some strange reason, Evelyn was feeling a bit lonely – something was nagging her.

After the celebration was over, Evelyn went for a stroll in the nature reserve. She needed to figure out why she was feeling lonely. All right, she was worried whether she would get along with her schoolmates … but that was only part of the problem. She was uncertain whether she was talented enough in martial arts … but that didn't explain the indescribable burden on her heart either. It was then that Evelyn remembered Victor, and the clouds in her mind suddenly cleared up. *One day, I've got to chase after Victor and finish him off … something my schoolmates probably wouldn't even think of!*

Kung fu was a choice for her schoolmates – they could fail, give up, or change career – but not for Evelyn. She didn't come here just to improve her fighting skills; she was here to be trained specifically for the fight against Victor, and she must succeed no matter what. For a moment, Evelyn imagined Victor to be a many-headed, multi-legged monster whom she had to defeat with kung fu kicks and punches … the prospect looked so bleak that she shivered and decided to head back to Student Lodge.

CHAPTER 9

First Lessons

Evelyn woke early on Monday morning. Walking out of Student Lodge and across campus, she saw four martial arts masters duelling on the beautiful lawn – they were punching, kicking, throwing knives and sparring with swords.

Really? thought Evelyn, wide-eyed. Filled with curiosity, she walked towards the duelling masters and realised they were high-tech 3D projections. These projections looked so real Evelyn would have thought they were real people, if she hadn't stood right next to them to investigate.

Evelyn then proceeded to her first class eagerly. At long last, the first day of martial arts learning had arrived. The classes in this university were known to be tough! First-year students had to learn eight styles of martial arts. They would be taught by martial arts masters from around the world, all of whom experts in their specific styles of duelling.

Professor Walker was their boxing and wrestling teacher. In the first lesson, he asked Evelyn and her classmates to meet him in the IT Centre's computer lab. The only words Professor Walker said that day were: "Experience is the best teacher!" A team of IT assistants then came in. They hooked each student up to a set of gadgets for a virtual reality experience of boxing-style hitting and being hit. It was an intense session, and afterwards, the students all felt very sore and tired.

Master Khan's Judo class took place in a specially designed underground hall: the floor was made of mat and the walls were covered in pads. Harsh and impatient, Khan brought four instructors with him and started teaching them Judo techniques right away. Their first lesson was about throws and breakfalls. After a brief demonstration, Master Khan and his four eagle-eyed instructors walked among the students shouting at them to correct their mistakes …

Master Takahashi was a Karate expert hailed from Japan. "First, I'm going to teach you unarmed techniques," he said, "after that, we're going to incorporate Samurai weapons to our training." Evelyn was wondering what Samurai had to do with Karate, except they both originated from Japan, when she heard heavy footsteps outside the classroom. She gasped when four people dressed in full Japanese armours barged in – they were carrying two wooden crates, and inside the crates were lots of long samurai swords! A sword fight demonstration swiftly followed: clunk, clunk, clunk … "See how beautiful it is to combine the art of Karate with Samurai swords," Master Takahashi said in a mesmerising voice. The whole class clapped – that was definitely impressive.

Master Lin, who everyone knew from the induction camp, was their Shaolin and Wing Chun kung fu teacher. His classroom was a hall full of stone statues of legendary kung fu masters, but he preferred to teach outdoor. With the aid of virtual reality glasses, they trained on a snowy peak in Tibet in the first lesson, and under the scorching sun in front of the Shaolin Temple in the second lesson. "A change of scenery, but the same old kung fu techniques!" Master Lin told them wisely.

By the end of the first week, Evelyn was missing Guillermo badly. So far, she had had lessons from Professor Walker, Master Khan, Master Takahashi and Master Lin. She couldn't help but wonder: *What about Guillermo's lesson?* And then, with much disappointment, she told herself: *Don't be stupid. He's the headmaster. Of course he's not going to teach first-year students.*

Evelyn's school life wasn't going as smoothly as she would have wanted either. There was Scarlett, that hateful girl who teased her at the start-of-term ceremony. Scarlett was relentless. She just kept telling everyone in the class how Evelyn was bitten like a "pig" in the Horror Cave, and advising people to stay away from this "idiot" at all costs!

Evelyn sighed. There was not much she could do for now. When the time came, she would prove herself. But until then …

It was lucky that Evelyn had her three animal friends to keep her company after classes every day. Evelyn had now given them names. Lola the panda warmed to her name almost immediately. She was growing so fast Evelyn expected this cuddly lady bear to tower over her in a few months. Hank the golden monkey took ages to learn his name. He no longer bit Evelyn while she fed him in his enclosure, which was a great improvement. Hank was bullied – Evelyn knew how it felt to be bullied – and she was glad to see him gradually putting the past behind him. Tyson the fox-leopard didn't care about names. He had his mind only on the raw, bloody meat Evelyn fed him. *Which is all right,* thought Evelyn; she would call him Tyson whether he liked it or not. Tyson had no family, just like herself. She sympathised with him.

Momoko, Lily, Heewon and Xiaojin hadn't spoken to Evelyn since the feast. Just as Evelyn thought they no longer wanted to be her friends, they approached her. It was Friday. They came together, all four of them smiling. What a surprise.

"Hi!" cried Evelyn, waving.

"Tomorrow's Saturday, and we're going to the hot spring on the other side of the mountain for a long, relaxing soak," Lily said blissfully. "Would you like to join us?"

Evelyn's heart sank: she was sure her metal core wasn't built for a long soak in hot water.

"It's very popular in Japan too," Momoko added cheerfully. "As you submerge your body in the hot mineral water, the heat will get under your skin and boost blood circulation."

Evelyn imagined her metal core being slowly heated up by the hot spring … *No, definitely not.*

"So, are you coming with us?" Xiaojin asked, her expression sincere.

"Er –" Evelyn didn't know what to say. She treasured the opportunity to go out with these girls, but why couldn't they do something more normal, like hiking on the mountains? Why did they have to soak themselves in hot water? In the end, Evelyn declined their invitation by saying she was not feeling well – a lame excuse obviously, but better than telling them about her metal core.

After her friends left, Evelyn felt rather lonely. The memory of Christmas dinner at Headmaster Mansion came back to her. She wondered wishfully, *When will Guillermo invite me again?* Next moment, she had come to her senses. *Don't be ridiculous,* she scolded herself, *you're just an insignificant first year. Why would he invite you but not the others?*

The second week got off to a bad start. Evelyn had not even left Student Lodge when she bumped into Scarlett. Scarlett shrieked in mock surprise the moment she saw Evelyn. Leaning towards her boyfriend – who was tall, muscular, and had blonde hair – she said in a loud voice so that everyone in the lounge could hear, "Gordon, I'd love to see you knock this idiot out in a fight!"

Gordon glanced at Evelyn. "I can finish her off with one punch," he sneered.

Evelyn stared at them. *I refuse to be provoked!* she thought with determination, and then walked on towards her Taekwondo class.

Their first Taekwondo lesson took place in a large sports hall within the university's sports centre. Evelyn was early, but Grandmaster Kim was earlier. A strict and unsmiling woman, the Taekwondo Grandmaster was already standing on stage – under a large Korean flag, and in front of several pots of Korean roses.

This was Grandmaster Kim's classroom, and it looked like a gallery. There were photos on the walls and videos displayed on hanging screens, each capturing a glorious Taekwondo moment at the Olympic Games over the years. Evelyn was wondering what was so special about the Olympic Games, when she spotted Grandmaster Kim in one of the photos: she had just won a gold medal in the Olympic Taekwondo event! She looked young … maybe ten years younger than now. In the video next to the photo, Kim could be seen standing proudly under a Korean flag, singing the national anthem, her eyes full of tears. Evelyn quickly looked up at the present Kim on stage, and caught the Taekwondo Grandmaster turning her head in the opposite direction. She must have been watching Evelyn a moment ago.

Once everyone had arrived, Grandmaster Kim began: "Some

people think Taekwondo is just sports – I'm here to enlighten you on its immense power. A good foundation in Taekwondo is important for both unarmed and armed fighting. In split-second emergency situations, Taekwondo makes the difference between life and death!"

The students looked at each other sceptically. Kim continued, "This morning, I'm going to teach you a few Taekwondo techniques. In the afternoon, we're going to have our first duel training. I expect you to apply what you learn in the morning to your afternoon duels. Understand?"

"Yes!" the whole class shouted, thrilled to hear that they would be duelling so soon.

"Good," said Grandmaster Kim, coming down from the stage. "Let's begin!" She finally gave them a little smile.

The morning session went well. In the afternoon, they returned for their duel training. Evelyn could see that blue mats had been placed on the wooden floor to mark the "duelling arena". After lecturing the first-year students about Taekwondo duelling rules and etiquettes, Grandmaster Kim asked, "Any volunteers?"

A few hands shot up in the air. Those who volunteered were all muscular young men, except for Evelyn.

"Ladies first," Kim said, picking Evelyn immediately. "One more girl please …"

"No girl? A boy then …"

This time, even those who volunteered earlier put down their hands. Scarlett grew impatient. She nudged her boyfriend and encouraged him in a shrill voice, "Go, Gordon. Take her down and get her out of the way. Don't let that idiot waste everyone's time!"

Gordon came forth with his head held high, his teeth

clenching tightly together. By the look of him, he did mean to knock Evelyn out with a single punch – to impress Scarlett mostly, but also to show off to the rest of the class.

Evelyn felt a chill down her spine: Gordon was a head taller than her, and it was difficult not to feel afraid. But her fear was mixed with hope; the chill in her spine was soon flooded out by warm blood pounding just under her skin. This was exactly what Evelyn had been waiting for – the opportunity to rise and shine, the chance to show the whole world she was a very promising martial arts fighter indeed!

Evelyn and Gordon put on the full Taekwondo gear: helmet, body armour and guards. They bowed under the watchful eyes of Grandmaster Kim.

"On the count of three," shouted Kim, acting as their referee.

"One." Gordon's eyes narrowed. He looked ruthless, like a bullfighter ready to slay his bull.

"Two." Evelyn briefly considered whether Gordon would start now to gain advantage over her – but no, he wouldn't because the whole class was watching. Evelyn waited with bated breath, any time now …

"Three!" the Grandmaster shouted and jumped out of the way. Evelyn leapt forward and kicked Gordon hard in the head!

She was quick as lightning, giving Gordon no time to respond. There was a loud bang as Gordon crashed to the ground. He went on to slide several metres on the floor, a long way out of the matted duelling arena, stopping only when he hit the wall behind. He lay on the ground cocooned in his Taekwondo helmet and armour, completely knocked out and not moving at all.

Evelyn heard sharp intakes of air … people gasping … people

uttering "Oh my God!" She froze, as shocked as her classmates: *It was just a kick!*

After a moment, Evelyn stepped forward to see if she could help Gordon in any way. Grandmaster Kim was already bending over him, checking his pulse. Evelyn heard her muttering, "Lucky you put on your helmet properly. Some guys never bother."

The Grandmaster then looked up at the gathering students. "Class dismissed! Make good use of this afternoon by practising what I taught you this morning." She noticed Evelyn squatting beside her. "You stay!" she ordered.

Two minutes later, a medical team came in with a stretcher and took Gordon away.

Scarlett was hysterical. "You almost killed him, you evil bitch," she pointed a quivering finger at Evelyn. "It was a false start!" she added furiously.

Lily frowned at Scarlett. "Grandmaster Kim, do you need student witnesses?" she asked politely. "It wasn't a false start. Some of us would like to be witnesses to the accident."

Behind Lily, Heewon was nodding vehemently.

But the Grandmaster wasn't listening. She glared at all the remaining students authoritatively. "I said class dismissed!" Turning to Evelyn, she raised her eyebrows and said coldly, "Follow me!"

Grandmaster Kim was quiet as she led Evelyn up a path through the mountain. Evelyn wanted to ask where they were going, but her mouth had gone dry. She tried to read from the unsmiling face of Kim, which was impossible. Evelyn wished she could tell the whole world there was no foul play, and she had won the duel fair and square … she doubted anyone would listen. One thing was for sure: *I'm going to be expelled, for almost killing a classmate!* Evelyn was also certain that this time, Ronald would terminate her. *He'll say I'm dangerously out of control.*

Evelyn couldn't go back to Ronald's factory, but where else could she go? She felt miserable. Tears were welling up in her eyes; she struggled to hold them back.

Grandmaster Kim stopped outside a two-storey stone house at the edge of a cliff. There was a sign next to the house that read "Master Chow's Office". Evelyn entered, expecting the worst.

CHAPTER 10

Fast Track to Success

"This is Master Chow," Kim introduced, "and this is Headmaster Guillermo."

Headmaster Guillermo? Evelyn, who had been staring at the ground, instantly looked up. She met Guillermo's eyes – he was frowning at her. *Oh no.* She quickly looked away.

"Master Chow, this is Evelyn." Kim continued.

Chow peered at Evelyn from behind his glasses.

"What happened?" he asked Kim.

"In my Taekwondo duelling lesson just now, Evelyn knocked a male student unconscious –"

"Is he badly hurt?" said Chow, raising an eyebrow.

"I don't think so. I have sent him to the University Hospital for a check-up, just to be sure."

"Good." Chow's expression was stern and unfathomable. "Evelyn, did you do it on purpose?"

"No, I didn't. I'm very sorry for what happened, and I'm willing to apologise to Gordon in person." Evelyn said quickly. She stared down at her fingers and started to pray. *Please, don't send me back to Ronald's factory …*

"Is there anything else you wish to say?" came Master Chow's voice.

"Yes …" Evelyn stammered. "I understand it is unforgivable to hurt a classmate … even if it is unintentional. I'm willing to accept punishment for today's accident. I promise not to kick so hard next time."

A moment's silence followed. Evelyn looked around Master Chow's office and noticed a large golden eagle gazing at her with fixed eyes. It was standing on the antique wood table by the window. She watched as it hopped out of a flap next to the window and soared into the sky, its wings fully stretched. The eagle looked so carefree that Evelyn imagined herself to follow it and fly out of this tension-filled room too …

"There's no need to feel sorry or apologise for winning a fair fight," said Master Chow suddenly, bringing Evelyn's wandering mind back to the present.

Oh. She blushed.

Grandmaster Kim chimed in, "It was definitely a fair fight. The boy Evelyn was duelling with was almost twice her size, and yet," Kim swallowed, still revelling in that incredible moment, "and yet, she managed to knock him out with a single kick. The boy didn't stand a chance: he crashed to the ground and slid several metres until he hit a wall!"

Evelyn was speechless. *Are you trying to say that I'm powerful, or else dangerous?*

"Evelyn, was that your first martial arts duel ever?" Guillermo prompted. He had been watching her intently.

"Yes, it was my first," she answered politely.

"Good heavens! Evelyn has no prior experience in martial arts?" Kim covered her mouth in shock. "I've never seen anything like this. The girl's a rare talent – this kind of speed and power is not something we can teach."

Chow nodded in agreement. "Kim, thanks for bringing Evelyn to my attention. I shall decide what's best for her and the university."

"Of course," said Kim. She stood up and left.

Master Chow suddenly smiled. "Ronald will be proud of you, Evelyn. Barely six weeks of age, you have already shown yourself to be a very talented fighter." Stroking his chin thoughtfully, he continued, "Guillermo, you are the best person I can think of to teach Evelyn and develop her full potential. Will you do it?"

Evelyn squirmed in her seat as Guillermo took his time to eye her appraisingly. He then answered in a cool and measured voice, "Yes, Chow, I will do whatever's necessary."

Master Chow took out a calligraphy brush and began writing a note. "I'm going to remove Evelyn from normal bachelor degree lessons," he said. "Instead, she's going to take one-to-one elite, private lessons from the headmaster."

Evelyn wanted to jump and punch the air: *Did he just call me an elite?* Half an hour ago, Evelyn had been so worried, thinking she was about to be expelled. Turned out, not only would she be staying on to learn martial arts but also she would be taking one-to-one lessons from none other than Guillermo! Evelyn couldn't believe her good luck: she felt like living in a dream.

"Evelyn, I need you to promise me that you'll train hard under Headmaster Guillermo," Chow said, still holding the calligraphy brush.

She glanced at Guillermo, and found him smiling encouragingly at her.

"I'll do anything Headmaster Guillermo asks me to do," Evelyn answered wholeheartedly, "as long as I don't need to go back to Ronald's factory!"

Chow sighed. "Ronald's a good man, and highly skilled. He created you. He just doesn't know how to treat people properly ..."

Back in Student Lodge, Evelyn's classmates had been waiting for her.

Lily jumped up and held Evelyn's hand. "Are you okay?" she asked, gazing into Evelyn's face with concern.

"Yes, I'm fine," Evelyn answered, feeling cheerful. She found a seat among her friends and shared her good news with them.

While Evelyn spoke, Scarlett could be seen lazing around on another couch. "Surely, the university can't allow someone as violent as her to stay on," she was telling her friends. When Scarlett learned that Evelyn had been accepted into the elite programme to train under the headmaster, no words could describe her jealousy – she ran away screaming and shrieking.

"Scarlett filmed your duel with Gordon, thought she could have a good laugh at you," Xiaojin told Evelyn.

Lily giggled. "Good for you, you completely ruined her plan!" She showed Evelyn the video. "Look at Gordon's face – he's the typical villain. And you, Evelyn, you're the super-woman ..."

"Now watch your kick," Heewon added admiringly. "It's almost like watching a superhero movie – the super-woman defeating the villain in a single, powerful blow! How did you do it, really?"

Evelyn simply smiled. She didn't want to encourage this talk about her "superhuman" talents. After all, it would expose her metal core which she had tried so hard to keep secret.

"Evelyn, when will we see you again, now that you're no longer going to classes with us?" Momoko asked her later that evening.

"We'll see each other in Student Lodge every evening," Evelyn answered sweetly.

"Right, of course! Goodnight, Evelyn."

At six the next morning, Evelyn set off for the lake where she would meet Guillermo for her first private lesson. The winter sky was still dark. Student Lodge was incredibly quiet: classes began at eight so other students were still asleep.

The lake was hard to find. Evelyn had to trek through the forest in darkness. On her way, she wondered, *What will Guillermo teach me?*

When Evelyn arrived, the sky was beginning to brighten up. Guillermo's broad shoulders were unmistakable. He was sitting in the cross-legged position, apparently meditating. There were two brown horses beside him. The horses were grazing leisurely on the overgrown grass. Evelyn widened her eyes – *that looks fun! Is Guillermo going to teach me horseback riding today?*

Guillermo jumped up from the ground. "Come here, Evelyn," he called out, giving her a reassuring smile. "We're going to practise kung fu on horseback."

"I've never ridden a horse," she told him honestly.

"I know you haven't. It'll take a bit of practice, but once you've learned to stay on the horse, I can teach you how to fight on horseback –"

One of the horses had stopped grazing and was staring at them. Evelyn looked at it anxiously.

"Won't the horses freak out?" she asked Guillermo.

"That's the point. You've got to control your horse and your moves at the same time," he said. "In real life situations, there are always going to be distractions while you fight, so it's best to start getting used to them."

At first, Evelyn couldn't even mount the horse: it was taller than she expected. Guillermo helped her climb onto it.

"Now tell your horse to go forward by squeezing your legs gently," he instructed.

Evelyn squeezed her legs – probably not gently enough – as the horse instantly got into an adrenaline-filled gallop. She was thrown off, landing heavily on the grass.

Guillermo led the horse back to her.

"Are you hurt?" he asked, offering his hand to pull her up.

Evelyn got up by herself. Brushing mud off her clothes, she bellowed, "I know! I know!"

"What do you know?" he asked curiously.

"I've just figured out how to ride!" said Evelyn, pointing determinedly at the horse.

"All right then." He came a step nearer to help her onto the horse, but Evelyn waved him away.

"Let me try it myself!" she said grumpily, leaping onto the horse with the right amount of force this time.

Guillermo smiled at her. "Now tell your horse to go forward."

Evelyn squeezed the horse with her legs – much more gently this time – and the horse started to trot. She could hear the clear, cheerful sounds of its hooves as they hit the ground with regular beat.

Guillermo clapped in appreciation. "That's it. You can do it. You are ready to fight!"

He jumped onto his horse and approached Evelyn. Evelyn held onto the rein tightly.

"Now try to punch me," Guillermo said when he had come close enough.

Evelyn hesitated, haunted by the memory of Gordon lying

unconscious after she kicked him. *But this is Guillermo, surely I won't be able to knock him out even if I want to.*

"What are you waiting for?" Guillermo shouted impatiently.

Evelyn punched him as hard as she could … but before her fist had even made contact with Guillermo, her horse had started to go wild, throwing her off balance. Hanging onto her horse precariously, Evelyn had to abandon punching and focused on getting back on the horse first. After a few clumsy moments, she managed to sit upright again.

Guillermo was watching her appraisingly.

"Again," he instructed. He didn't come close this time. "Punch me!"

Evelyn focused: she trotted her horse towards Guillermo and then punched him in the stomach. The punch wasn't as fast or powerful as Evelyn would have wanted – Guillermo's body didn't even twitch under her blow – but she did manage not to fall off the horse.

"Good job, Evelyn," Guillermo praised. "Come down. I'm going to teach you some kicks and throws …"

They trained till four in the afternoon. Afterwards, Evelyn said goodbye to Guillermo and led the two horses back to the university's stable.

Evelyn had been keeping up with her volunteering work in the nature reserve after lessons with Guillermo. She was taking on more responsibilities now. Apart from Lola the panda, Hank the monkey and Tyson the fox-leopard, Evelyn had also been keeping an eye out for a pregnant panda who was due to give birth. Seeing Evelyn's enthusiasm, Director Zhang had given Evelyn an alarm which would alert her when that pregnant panda went into labour.

One night, Evelyn was dozing off in her room when the panda alarm beeped and vibrated urgently. Without second thoughts, she dashed out of Student Lodge and raced towards the nature reserve. She got to the animal hospital just in time. Looking through a glass panel, Evelyn could see four vets were on hand to deliver the baby pandas. Director Zhang was also there, supervising.

A pink little head had already poked out of the panda mum's bottom, and before long, the most miraculous thing happened: the first baby came out completely, followed by the second. The panda mum had smoothly given birth to twins! Evelyn had never seen anything quite like them: the baby pandas were pink, blind, and incredibly tiny – a far cry from any panda Evelyn had seen in the nature reserve.

The vets cleansed the two babies carefully, giving one of them to the mother and putting the other into a glass incubator. Director Zhang then opened the door and waved Evelyn in.

"First time witnessing a panda giving birth?" he smiled at her tiredly.

"Yes, it was amazing. The panda babies are so cute and tiny!" Evelyn gushed.

"They are also very fragile. That's why I don't usually allow student volunteers to go near the baby pandas until the cubs are at least two months old," said Director Zhang.

"Oh," Evelyn muttered, feeling disappointed. She had been hoping to take care of those cute panda cubs.

Director Zhang gazed at her thoughtfully. "Having said that, I see you are different, Evelyn. You have some experience with difficult animals. I can give you special permission to care for the baby pandas … if you want to."

Evelyn was delighted. "Yes, definitely! I'll be careful and

gentle around the precious babies!"

Director Zhang nodded. "Good, I'll count you in." Looking at his gold wristwatch, he yawned, "It's late, Evelyn. You'd better go back to your room and have a nap before lessons start in the morning."

Chinese New Year was fast approaching. Evelyn could hardly believe it when she realised she had been living in China for almost two months. She was flourishing both in her volunteering work and her private lessons with Guillermo. Adding to Evelyn's joyous mood was the beautiful Chinese New Year decorations that had been put up around campus and in the nature reserve. Everywhere she went, Evelyn could see Chinese red lanterns that varied in shapes from spheres to lotuses and even unicorns. On doors and walls, there were New Year couplets – stylish calligraphy on red paper; and on windows, there were auspicious red paper cuttings – showing animals or mythical creatures. Potted tangerine trees had also sprung up in and around buildings, often with red packets attached to the branches as though they were part of the plant.

The week before Chinese New Year, Guillermo gave Evelyn yet another reason to feel joyful.

"That's all for basic techniques," he announced, looking immensely proud of her. "It's time for you to move on to advanced techniques and weapon training."

"What weapons will I be wielding?" Evelyn asked eagerly.

"Hmm … Follow me!"

Guillermo took her to Kung Fu Tower, a pagoda-style building. The ground floor was an impressive hall where statues of legendary masters were displayed side-by-side with holograms of their signature moves. Evelyn followed Guillermo to the basement, stopping in front of a polished metal door. Guillermo pressed his finger on the keypad and the door slid open.

"Welcome to the grand kung fu armoury," he said mysteriously.

Wow. Evelyn had never seen so many weapons so awesomely displayed. There were swords, spears, maces, axes, tridents, shields, clubs and staffs. And they were in different colours: gold, silver, bronze, jade green …

"You may choose any weapon that your heart desires," Guillermo told her warmly. "After you have chosen, we're going to the IT Centre to practise using that specific weapon."

"Got it!" Evelyn answered smartly. She felt like a warrior today. Looking around, Evelyn found what she wanted – a long, silver sword with a finely crafted leather sheath! She took it down immediately. Clutching the magnificent sword to her chest, Evelyn left Kung Fu Tower in a buoyant mood.

She followed Guillermo to the IT Centre. There was an entire floor in the IT Centre dedicated to high-tech weapon training. Stepping out of the elevator, Evelyn could see plenty of training rooms separated by glass walls. She got into one of these rooms with Guillermo. The glass walls turned out to be digital screens: they darkened up the moment she closed the door. The screen in front of her instantly recognised the weapon she had chosen and began explaining to her how to use it. Evelyn was then told to test her weapon. There must be sensors installed everywhere in this room, because the screens were able to point out her mistakes and give immediate feedback.

After the testing, Evelyn moved on to practical training. This part was more interactive – the difficulty level was adjustable, and there were moving targets for her to hit at. The screens in the room acted like Evelyn's coach, providing a detailed analysis of her performance – her power and precision in sword fighting, the time and energy she had expended, mistakes and fixes to her movement …

Guillermo left while Evelyn learned to use the sword, but returned by nightfall to see how she was doing. He had brought with him a freshly baked chocolate cake to cheer her up. Evelyn was feeling rather irritable after the difficult training. Her whole body was aching. She stuffed the entire cake down her throat without chewing. The sweet food, unfortunately, failed to lift her mood.

"Guillermo, what good are weapons if Victor doesn't even have a body? How am I going to fight Victor with martial arts?" she asked, frustrated.

Guillermo stroked his chin and gazed at Evelyn, his eyes boring into hers. "Victor's got many evil accomplices with bodies, so that's how martial arts will come in useful. And the mental qualities you gain from martial arts training? You will need them to pursue Victor when the time comes."

Evelyn stared back at him moodily. "Why me? Life's so unfair!" she complained, and started to weep.

At first, Guillermo watched her with a guarded expression. And then, in a rare gesture of affection, he gave her a little hug, whispering in her ear, "You know, Evelyn, you are not alone. I'm with you."

On Chinese New Year Day, Evelyn woke up to an intense smell of turnip cake wafting from the corridor. She went to the kitchen and found the place filled with white flavoursome steam. Lily, Heewon and Momoko were making a lavish Chinese meal.

There was food all over the laminate worktop. A huge turnip cake was sitting in a bamboo steamer on the stove.

"Happy Chinese New Year, Evelyn!"

"Happy Chinese New Year! Where's Xiaojin?" Evelyn asked.

"She went home last night," said Lily. Pointing to the stove, she added, "The turnip cake will be ready in fifteen minutes. Would you like to try some?"

Evelyn shook her head. "Sorry, Lily, I'm in a hurry. I've got to help out in the nature reserve. It's going to be a busy day there."

Heewon, who had been leaning against the fridge, jumped up suddenly.

"Good luck in the nature reserve, Evelyn. See you later!"

Even though it was early morning, the nature reserve's Visitor Centre was already quite crowded. Families were standing around the hologram projections of animals, chatting loudly. There were children running up and down the state-of-the-art glass building, playing hide-and-seek. Evelyn had to stop abruptly when a red-haired boy almost ran into her while being chased by his Chinese playmate.

Evelyn passed the Visitor Centre and headed to the panda nursery, where she spent the morning caring for the baby pandas. It was past midday when she finished all her work. She was removing her uniform when the security alarms went off and a public announcement blared:

"Ladies and gentleman, an emergency has been reported. The nature reserve is now closed. Please leave immediately –"

What emergency? thought Evelyn, walking out of the panda nursery dubiously.

A herd of deer was galloping down the slope; Evelyn swiftly

stepped out of the way to avoid being knocked over. People were running in all directions, shouting and screaming. One gentleman saw Evelyn standing by the side of the road and urged her in a tense voice, "The lion's coming, you'd better run!"

The lion? Evelyn frowned. She knew as a fact that there was not a single lion living in the entire nature reserve.

Evelyn was hesitating when another group of tourists came running in her direction. They were led by a guide in uniform, and next to the tourists, a dozen hedgehogs were running for their lives. Evelyn stared at the hedgehogs.

"Leave!" the tour guide shouted at Evelyn in a rough voice. "Animals out of enclosure. Leave now!"

Evelyn froze as it suddenly dawned on her –

"The fox-leopard!" she cried out. *Tyson's used to living in his enclosure … who knows whether he'll tear the whole place apart once he's loose?*

"Leave," the tour guide repeated earnestly. "You don't want to be standing here when the fox-leopard comes charging down the road!"

Evelyn had no time to explain. She raced towards the fox-leopard enclosure without another word. If there was anyone who stood a chance of stopping Tyson – it would be she, Evelyn.

CHAPTER 11

Attack on the Nature Reserve

Evelyn leapt through fences and bushes to get to the fox-leopard enclosure. On her way, she could hear the screams of frantic tourists running away from the rumoured "lion". She found a child wandering alone in the bushes, and had to gently push him back to his worried parents.

Evelyn also encountered a herd of five stampeding rhinoceros – uniformed keepers on electric motorcycles were trying to catch up with them. The rhinoceros were unstoppable. Evelyn watched in disbelief as they knocked down stone walls, trampled all over the exotic flower garden and broke into the Butterfly Conservatory. She could hear glass shattering even from afar.

As Evelyn reached the most popular part of the nature reserve – a traditional Chinese street with souvenir shops and restaurants on both sides – she found the usually crowded place eerily quiet. It was like a ghost town. People were hiding in the shops and restaurants. They had barricaded the entrances with chairs, tables and even brooms. Evelyn could see panicked faces pressing against the windows, looking out for escaped animals.

The tourists gasped when they saw Evelyn walking on the empty street. Since Evelyn had just removed her uniform, they had no idea she worked in the nature reserve. The tourists began to wave, knock on windows and make various gestures to Evelyn, desperate to get her out of the dangerous street.

Evelyn ignored all the distracting faces. She had an important task to do: *All right, where's Tyson?*

Suddenly, Evelyn sensed a beast falling out of the sky. She looked up instinctively, using her enhanced eyes and brain to see things in slow motion …

It was Tyson. He had just jumped out of a tree. This moment, he was still in mid-air; next moment, he had landed in front of Evelyn with a thud. There was a bloody squirrel dangling from his mouth. Tyson was staring coldly at Evelyn – he didn't seem his usual self.

Evelyn froze. Bad memories came rushing back: the last time she faced Tyson without her special alloy suit, it was catastrophic, and that was despite having a metal fence between them.

Praying that Tyson wasn't going to finish her off, Evelyn summoned up all her courage and commanded bravely, "Go back, Tyson!"

To Evelyn's amazement, Tyson obeyed. He turned round and sprinted uphill back to his enclosure.

Evelyn immediately called the keepers at the fox-leopard enclosure, telling them Tyson was on his way. The head keeper went to check the live visuals from the surveillance cameras.

"There he is!" he shouted. Tyson had just returned on his own.

Breathing a sigh of relief, Evelyn punched the air triumphantly. *Yes!* She felt great to have put the nature reserve's deadliest predator back to his place.

But her good feeling didn't last long.

On her way back to the main campus, Evelyn sensed a tiny movement under a collapsed brick wall. Fearing that someone might be trapped underneath, Evelyn activated her infrared eyes to scan through the rubble. Fortunately, no one was trapped under the rubble, though there was a bird – heavily injured, and probably beyond her help.

Evelyn sighed. She was about to turn away when the bird started to cry in a pitiful yet persistent way – it was making a valiant effort to hold on to life. The cries resonated through Evelyn's heart and mind. There was no way she could just walk away and leave the bird to die. Evelyn wanted to help: she knew she had to take the bird with her and do whatever she could to save it.

Evelyn dug up the bird from the rubble, and was slightly disappointed to find that it was just an ordinary bird – quite small, and not particularly beautiful. She looked into the eyes of the injured bird; the bird looked straight back with stoical calm. Suddenly, Evelyn was overcome by an immense, ineffable feeling that this was no ordinary bird after all. *This bird's special* … Evelyn felt a sudden burst of energy as all the senses in her body were trying to make the same point at the same time! Deep in her heart, there was a curious, otherworldly feeling that somehow, she was destined to find this bird. No amount of words could ever describe her peculiar feelings right now.

Holding the bird safely in her hand, Evelyn started to run. She took a shortcut towards the animal hospital in the nature reserve, crashing through bushes along the way.

The Sichuan Animal Hospital was a futuristic-looking complex located by a peaceful lake. It was the flagship animal hospital in southwestern China – funded by the government, equipped with the most advanced medical technologies, and staffed by top veterinary surgeons. Evelyn felt lucky to be living within walking distance of such a good animal hospital: her special bird deserved the best medical attention.

On arrival, the animal hospital was very crowded. Evelyn had to stand on tiptoe to see where she should take her bird. She then wove through people and animals to make a dash for the admission counter.

"This bird's dying. It's urgent!" Evelyn told the duty nurse in a loud, anxious voice, presenting her injured bird delicately.

The duty nurse took a cursory glance at the bird.

"We are full at the moment." Her tone was business-like. "Your bird has low conservation value. I suggest you let it go … let it rest in peace …"

What? Evelyn was in shock. *But this bird can't die – she's special, like no other, and must be saved! How can I make you understand?*

"Please," Evelyn pleaded, "my bird's so small. It won't take up much space."

The duty nurse was unimpressed.

"I can euthanise the bird for you if you don't want to watch it suffer," she said in a cool, callous way.

"May I see an animal doctor, please?" Evelyn asked, her eyes red.

"All our doctors are busy at the moment," the nurse raised her voice impatiently.

"May I see the manager?" Evelyn persisted, making a last-ditch effort to save her special bird.

"No, you may not!" the nurse barked at her. "Don't be selfish! There has been a major incident in the nature reserve.

Our hands are full of rare and endangered species."

Tears began to streak down Evelyn's face. The nurse stared at her and tried to be nicer.

"Are you a student from the kung fu university? If this bird's your pet, I suggest you replace it with a healthy one. You know, this kind of bird is not difficult to find."

Evelyn glared at the nurse, picked up her dying bird, and stormed out of the animal hospital. She felt so helpless. *If I can't even save my little bird, how am I going to save the whole world from Victor?*

Returning to the main campus, Evelyn was temporarily distracted by what she saw – some runaway animals had got into the university. She passed a group of male students who were desperately trying to corner a pair of rhinoceros. It wasn't easy, as the rhinoceros were very ill-tempered, thrashing around violently. Panting and sweating, the group of students barely managed to hold them back.

Further down the path, another group of students had caught three Sichuan golden monkeys in separate nets. Amid the noisy squeaking of monkeys, Evelyn could hear a girl calling the nature reserve urging them to "come and bring the monkeys home as soon as possible".

There was even a panda on campus – frightened, but unharmed. A group of chatty girls had gathered around the panda, eager to feed and pat it. Evelyn shook her head. *Poor panda …*

She was wandering aimlessly around campus when someone walked up to her.

"Evelyn, what are you doing here? Your eyes are so red, have you been crying?"

Evelyn recognised the voice immediately: it was Guillermo.

"Are you hurt? Why are you holding a bird?" His words came out in a rush. He sounded anxious.

Evelyn stared up at him as tears rolled down her face. She was so overwhelmed with emotions she struggled to hold herself together: Evelyn wanted … needed … to save her special bird … it was such a small task, and yet she couldn't do it … no one cared about her, or her bird … she felt so useless, so unworthy …

Guillermo took her hand and squeezed it gently. "What's wrong, Evelyn? Tell me."

"This bird," she said in between sobs, gazing at the dying creature in her hand with pity, "I found it under a collapsed wall. It's small but special. I can feel it with all my heart!"

"Right," Guillermo murmured softly, patting her shoulder. He was all ears.

"My heart tells me this bird and I are destined to be together," Evelyn continued, "so I took it to the animal hospital to be healed. The nurse there refused to take in my bird … said it has low conservation value … she even threatened to euthanise my bird!"

"That's cruel." Guillermo gazed at her, his expression sincere.

Evelyn was now shaking with grief and anger.

"You see, this very special bird is going to die, and it's all my fault – I'm so useless, so worthless –"

She vented her frustration by beating herself up with her free hand. Guillermo frowned and knocked her hand out of the way.

"Don't!" he told her firmly. "I have an idea."

Evelyn stared at him dazedly. "You do?"

"Positive. Follow me!"

Guillermo took Evelyn to the nearest building, where he

printed off a formal letter bearing the school crest and letterhead of Yin-Yang Martial Arts University. He took out a fountain pen from his pocket and added a few lines of Chinese words.

"We can't argue about the bird's conservation value," Guillermo uttered as he wrote, "so let's say this bird has great symbolic value to the university."

He signed his name at the bottom and folded the letter.

"Here!" he pushed the letter into Evelyn's hand. "Take your bird to the animal hospital again. Show them this letter. I'll be very surprised if they refuse to admit your bird this time."

Evelyn sprinted towards the animal hospital. She had one hand around her precious bird, the other clutching Guillermo's letter.

The duty nurse was still there. She gaped at Evelyn when she saw her, with the bird … again! The nurse was going to throw Evelyn out – in fact she had already opened her mouth – when Evelyn threw Guillermo's letter onto the desk. The colourful yin-yang crest was particularly eye-catching in the sterile environment of the hospital.

The nurse paused to read the letter.

"You're very determined, aren't you?" she said, narrowing her eyes. "You even got the headmaster to vouch for you."

Evelyn's bird was admitted to the animal hospital straight away. It was given a high-tech medical incubator to recuperate in. After a short wait, it was attended by several veterinary surgeons.

"How's it?" Evelyn asked the consultant – a grey-haired, Chinese man in his fifties.

The consultant smiled at Evelyn kindly. "Your bird's a she, and she's a lucky bird. She's going to make a full recovery."

Evelyn smiled back. She was feeling rather cheerful when she received an unexpected message from Lily: "Heewon's in the hospital. We are with her now."

Is she badly hurt? thought Evelyn, alarmed. Heewon volunteered in the Reptile House, and Evelyn knew the creatures there could be quite nasty!

Evelyn rushed to University Hospital at once. She found Heewon in a rather bad shape: she had broken an arm, and both her legs were heavily bandaged.

"Heewon! How are you feeling?"

Lily and Momoko quickly made room for Evelyn to come closer.

"Actually, not bad," Heewon answered with a tired smile. "I tripped over a snake, that's all."

"You what?" Evelyn gaped at her, perplexed.

"I was volunteering at the Reptile House," Heewon explained. "It was around midday when the alarms went off and the vivariums unlocked themselves – the snakes were slithering out!"

"Oh no," Evelyn gasped.

"There were more than a hundred snakes in my section. It was impossible to hold them back. All I could do was to go around telling tourists to exit calmly –"

"That's very brave of you."

"The next thing I knew, I had tripped on a Chinese Water Snake. I jumped up to avoid falling on the snake –"

Evelyn's mouth dropped open. "And then what happened?"

Heewon grimaced. "Today has to be the worst day of my life! First, I broke my left arm colliding with the stone wall. Then, I got stabbed on both legs falling on a shattered vase." She sounded breathless.

"That's horrible!" Evelyn exclaimed. Pointing a shaky finger at Heewon's legs, she said, "I guess you needed a lot of stitches afterwards."

Heewon nodded. "Too many to be counted," she answered drily.

"We'll take care of you while you recover," Momoko promised.

"Thanks," Heewon sighed.

There was a moment's silence as they enjoyed each other's company.

"Look, a new message from Master Chow to the whole school!" Lily shouted suddenly.

They squeezed together around Heewon to look at Lily's screen.

"A special gathering regarding today's attack on the nature reserve – Great Hall, six o'clock," Lily read the message out.

"An attack? D-do you think …" Momoko stuttered, too nervous to continue.

"Do you think Victor's behind today's attack?" Lily finished the sentence for her.

Momoko nodded her head gratefully.

Evelyn was dumbfounded. This was the first time she had heard her friends talk about Victor. "Victor?" she muttered to herself, but Lily heard her.

"Yes, Victor, the Shapeless Evil – didn't you read the news, Evelyn? Everyone's talking about Victor and his worldwide attacks –"

"You know what they said in the news the other day?" Heewon added darkly. "Victor has become so dangerous that … nowhere's safe now, and no one's spared!"

Evelyn's mouth dropped open. To think that Ronald created her to fight this ever-growing evil called Victor! How on earth was she going to defeat Victor?

Momoko looked as stunned as Evelyn.

"I really thought we would be spared … tucked away in a remote mountain in China …"

"Apparently, not remote enough for Victor," said Lily sourly.

Heewon sighed, "It's a shame I can't go to the special gathering this evening."

"Don't worry, I can definitely make a recording for you," Evelyn told her brightly.

"You are so nice!" Heewon cried out, clasping Evelyn's arm with her uninjured hand.

Evelyn wished Heewon a speedy recovery and said goodbye to her friends. After that, she returned to the main campus, making a detour to the nature reserve.

The path through the nature reserve was a mess: there were collapsed walls, fallen trees, New Year decorations with dirty footprints on them, and all kinds of personal belongings left behind by panicked tourists.

Evelyn felt a bit better when she saw that robot cleaners had been sent out to clear up the mess. The computer system seemed to be up and running too. Overhead, Evelyn could hear the faint whirring sounds from infrared sensors and surveillance cameras as they restarted. Around her, biometric keypads to enter enclosures, previously turned dark, had lighted up again.

Evelyn arrived for the special gathering at a quarter to six. The Great Hall was already packed with students. There were no tables or chairs this time. Everyone was standing, and the atmosphere was highly charged.

Evelyn was going to find Lily and Momoko in the crowd when she sensed people gawking at her. She looked around and was surprised to see herself on people's electronic devices! A lot of students were watching her "fight" against Tyson – videos filmed and shared by tourists hiding in shops and restaurants while she handled the beast. A few students had even paused their videos at that "David vs Goliath" moment when Evelyn stood in front of Tyson on a deserted street. They were looking Evelyn up and down, comparing the person in the video with her real person.

These people were freaking Evelyn out: she needed to flee! She thought she had better wait outside the hall until Master Chow arrived.

Lowering her head, Evelyn made a dash for the exit. She was halfway through the hall when a tall, muscular man walked into her path. Evelyn was so focused on fleeing she failed to react in time …

She knew it was Guillermo the moment she crashed into his warm body. This was so embarrassing, especially with all eyes in the hall watching her.

"Hi," Evelyn mumbled, looking up at Guillermo.

Guillermo was grinning. "How's your beloved bird, Evelyn?" he asked warmly.

"Er … she's doing fine," Evelyn stammered, feeling self-conscious. "The doctor says she's going to make a full recovery."

"Excellent!" Guillermo cheered, gazing into her eyes. "I heard what you did with the fox-leopard, Evelyn. I'm so proud of you."

"It's nothing," Evelyn answered, blushing scarlet.

Guillermo gave her a pat on the shoulder and headed to the stage.

After her brief encounter with Guillermo, Evelyn felt a bit light-headed. Luckily –

"Evelyn!" Momoko and Lily were calling and waving at her. Evelyn quickly joined them.

"Why didn't you tell us about the fox-leopard when we were with Heewon?" Momoko asked, pouting slightly. "We have only just learned about your feat from the other students!"

"I was …" Evelyn tried to explain, but was at a loss for words.

Lily spared her the trouble.

"Evelyn, you are incredible!" Her voice was filled with admiration. "Holding off that fox-leopard all by yourself – I doubt anyone else could have done better."

Momoko broke into a smile too and added, "Honestly, I couldn't believe my eyes when I first saw that video. Evelyn, what you did was a miracle –"

The large bronze bell at the entrance of the Great Hall suddenly rang out, its sound reverberating around the hall. Evelyn looked up to see Master Lin holding the hammer, ready to strike again if the first bell was not enough to call for everyone's attention.

He didn't need to. The babble died away instantly, and silence reigned.

Master Chow was standing in the middle of the stage, his expression solemn.

"Thank you for coming to this special gathering," he said in a booming voice. "Today, Victor, also known as the Shapeless Evil, has attacked us."

Quietness shrouded the hall. Students looked at each other – angry, but not surprised.

"At around noon today, Victor hacked into the central

computer system of the nature reserve, releasing the animals there and causing much chaos."

The whole school listened with rapt attention.

"I would like to thank those of you who helped in the evacuation of tourists and capture of runaway animals. I applaud you, for showing much bravery and gallantry. In particular, I would like to thank Evelyn Smith, a first-year student, for leading the dangerous fox-leopard away from tourists. Her selfless act has certainly saved a lot of lives today."

All eyes were on Evelyn once more. She squeezed herself between Momoko and Lily. Evelyn had blushed many times since entering the Great Hall, but none as intensely as this time – her face felt like it was on fire.

"Tonight, I have an important message to all of you: As practitioners of martial arts, we are trained in both our mind and our body. In view of Victor's recent attacks worldwide, we must stay strong and fight evil together – and never give up, no matter what!" Master Chow concluded with force and conviction.

Around Evelyn, the whole school responded with spirited shouts and chants. Students began to clap in a rhythmic way. The clapping lasted for over a minute.

Refreshment was served afterwards. Evelyn didn't want to linger. Excusing herself from Momoko and Lily, who were both very understanding, she ran back to Student Lodge before everybody else. It had been a long day, and after all the surreal things that had happened today, Evelyn really needed to take a break and calm herself down.

CHAPTER 12

Training for Battle

Victor's attack on the nature reserve made a lot of students realise just how imminent Victor's threat was. Suddenly, the whole school was practising martial arts harder than ever. It was now clear to everyone that even though Victor was shapeless, his evil effects could take many forms – for example, in the form of dangerously out-of-control animals. Martial arts would then come in useful.

The training rooms in the IT Centre now opened twenty-four hours a day in response to students' demand. At the grand kung fu armoury in Kung Fu Tower, an unprecedented amount of weapons were borrowed by students in preparation for the fight against Victor.

Meanwhile, Evelyn was also training for battle. Her private lessons with Guillermo were no longer confined to the real world, but extended into the computer world. In her first lesson after Chinese New Year, Guillermo connected both of them to a curious-looking machine.

"Where are we going?" asked Evelyn.

"We're going into the computer simulated world … to a tropical island," he answered, giving the whole set-up a final check.

Evelyn smiled to herself. *Wow, that sounds warm and relaxing.*

Guillermo's finger was now hovering above a large green button.

"Are you ready?" he asked, grinning.

"Definitely!" Evelyn shouted. She was in high spirits.

Boom! Evelyn found herself surrounded by water – she was in a sea.

Oh my God, I don't know how to swim! Not wanting to give up so soon, Evelyn decided to punch and kick the water as if it was just another nasty opponent in a duel. Her strategy didn't work at all, and she was sinking fast. The sky was disappearing from her eyes, and darkness was closing in …

A powerful arm pulled her up to the surface.

"Evelyn, you are supposed to swim!" Guillermo yelled at her. He looked exasperated.

Evelyn held onto his muscular arm and gasped for air. She couldn't believe she almost drowned.

"I have never swum before," she spat, upset.

Guillermo shook his head and sighed, "All right then, watch me."

"Don't leave me!" Evelyn screamed in horror.

"Hold on to my arm. We're going back to shore together," he said as he began swimming forward. "The first step towards learning to swim is not to fight the water."

Evelyn tried her best to stay still – *not to fight the water* – allowing herself to glide through the water instead. As they neared shore, she saw a beautiful beach awaiting them.

Leaving two distinct sets of footprints on the sand, they arrived at the base of a cliff. Evelyn looked up nervously.

"What now?"

Guillermo pointed to some sturdy ropes hanging by the cliff. "We're going to climb up."

"Why?" Evelyn grumbled. The cliff was very steep, rugged and looked no fun at all.

"It's a basic skill in the computer world – climbing walls and cliffs," Guillermo explained, running his fingers through the harness.

Evelyn snorted.

"Trust me, you're going to like it up there," he added, winking.

Evelyn was suspicious at first, but as it turned out, climbing was a totally different experience from swimming. She was actually good at it. The footholds might be small, and the balance was precarious, but Evelyn managed to keep a firm grip on the rocks nonetheless. She realised she could almost pull herself up the entire cliff by her hands alone. She dared not look down though – the sheer drop was bloodcurdling.

"You're very talented," Guillermo patted her shoulder as she reached the top of the cliff. "I'm impressed."

Whatever confidence Evelyn lost in the sea, she regained through her satisfying climb. She felt so proud of herself. Looking ahead, Evelyn saw a large piece of grassland, where deer and zebras were grazing. And further beyond –

"A castle!" she screamed with delight. All of a sudden, she started running towards it like an excited child.

"Watch out!" Guillermo shouted, catching Evelyn's arm just in time to yank her back.

Evelyn paled: in front of her was a deep, wide fissure! How she could have missed something this obvious, Evelyn was too ashamed to reflect upon. In any case, one more step, and she would have toppled right into the abyss.

Since the danger was over, Evelyn put on a brave face and jumped across the deep, wide fissure with dogged determination …

She made it!

"Nice jump, Evelyn. You're a natural," Guillermo praised her.

Evelyn smiled, her mood instantly lifted. Making sure that the path was indeed clear, she resumed running towards the castle. Soon, they were standing outside its walls.

"Are we going to explore the castle?" she asked energetically.

"Maybe next time, when we go on a treasure hunt," Guillermo answered. "This time, we are merely passing through."

Guillermo climbed over the castle wall with his bare hands. Evelyn followed his lead, eager to prove herself. They ran on the roofs of a row of outer cottages. Reaching the grand main structure, Guillermo began jumping from tower to tower. Evelyn kept up well, and was able to emulate every jump he made, until she had to stop suddenly.

"Are you kidding me?" Evelyn exclaimed, aghast.

She found herself facing a volcano – a live, ash-blowing, lava-flowing volcano! It was huge too, and so volatile. The volcano looked like it could have a massive eruption any moment.

"Last challenge of the day: Jump across the volcano!" Guillermo announced in a mysterious voice.

"How is that even possible?" asked Evelyn, absolutely clueless.

"How was it possible you ran on rooftops and jumped from tower to tower?" Guillermo prompted her. "Welcome to the computer world, where much more is possible than you think."

"What if I fall into the volcano?" Evelyn blurted out.

"Don't worry, you won't die," Guillermo answered in a soothing tone.

"But how exactly am I going to jump across?" Evelyn continued, not the least enlightened.

"It takes practice to be perfect … basically, you focus your mind on the opposite side, and you jump. Watch me."

Evelyn watched in awe: Guillermo's jump was so mighty it was as if he flew right over the volcano. He was now standing on the other side of the volcano. Through the heat and smoke, Evelyn could see him waving at her, signalling her to make the jump.

Evelyn stared into the crater, which was fiery to say the least. She had her doubts, but was willing to make a leap of faith. She took a hundred steps back, and then started running towards the volcano … faster and faster she ran … As she reached the edge, she cried "Hooray!" and jumped as far as she could … she kept running in the air to maintain her momentum …

Evelyn never made it. Missing the opposite edge of the crater, she fell right into the volcano.

At first, Evelyn was surrounded by lava: the scorching heat was unbearable, and she thought she was going to be burnt to death! As Evelyn fell deeper, the volcano seemed to disappear. She found herself inside a pitch-dark tunnel, the cool air rushing up her face was a welcome relief. Finally, Evelyn crashed to the bottom of the volcano, which was dimly-lit and filled with rocks. *Ouch*. What a fall!

Guillermo was by her side within seconds.

"Are you all right?" he asked.

Evelyn grimaced – her knees were aching.

"I really thought I was going to make it!" she whimpered,

looking up at the top of the crater longingly.

"You'll make it eventually. Like I said, practice makes perfect," Guillermo encouraged her. "We've made a lot of progress today. Let's get back."

He held his hand out to her. Evelyn took it … and they were back in the real world, hooked up to wires and devices in a private room in the IT Centre.

One day after lesson, Guillermo said, "Come with me, Evelyn, I want to show you something."

"What?" she asked, rather grumpily. It had been a rough session in the computer world, and Evelyn's body was still aching from her many falls.

Guillermo regarded her with sympathy. "Don't worry, we are done with the training. It's something real … follow me!"

Guillermo took her to a lake outside campus, where they were surrounded by wilderness. There was nothing of particular interest here. Evelyn grew impatient.

"Where is it?"

"It's under the lake," he answered secretively, pointing to a set of stone steps hidden behind some trees on their right.

"Oh," said Evelyn. Bemused, she followed Guillermo down the steps into a dark tunnel beside the lake. The first hundred steps or so were very slippery and felt downright dangerous. If Evelyn had been alone, she would definitely have turned back. But Guillermo was in front of her, leading the way, and Evelyn knew she shouldn't complain.

As they reached deeper – Evelyn believed they had to be under the lake now – the tunnel widened up into a cave. It was exotically beautiful here. The stalactites and stalagmites were so massive they joined up to form columns. Multi-coloured lights were installed in the walls, shining around in a mysterious way.

There was a wooden door at the bottom of the stone steps, opening up to –

"Wow." Evelyn found herself in an enormous, dome-shaped chamber. Through the glass ceiling, she could see the lake, and rays of sunshine which had penetrated through water. Around her, robots of different shapes and sizes were doing excavation and construction work. There were also loads of furniture and high-tech gadgets piled up against the wall.

"This looks like a huge project!" she cried out, awestruck.

"This is our brand-new virtual reality computer lab," Guillermo declared in a visionary tone, "a state-of-the-art facility allowing up to a hundred and fifty students to enter the computer world together to fight Victor."

"That's impressive!" said Evelyn heartily.

"I designed the whole structure myself," Guillermo added.

"How did you do it?" she asked, wide-eyed.

Guillermo shrugged. "The key is to create three-dimensional models which are as clear and detailed as possible. After that, everything should automatically go as planned." He pointed at the robots and machines which were hard at work.

"Ingenious! Do all the teachers know about this project?" asked Evelyn.

Guillermo chuckled. "Of course not. Master Chow knows, I know; and now, you know. Just three people altogether." He patted Evelyn's shoulder amiably. "This place is far from finished. Let's come back when it's ready to use."

Evelyn waved goodbye to Guillermo and set off for her volunteer work. The nature reserve was closed for a week after Victor's attack, for essential maintenance, but it had since reopened, and tourists were flooding back.

It was lucky that Lola, Hank and Tyson were now requiring less of Evelyn's attention – Lola had made some panda friends, while Hank and Tyson had become a lot better at obeying commands – giving Evelyn the time she needed to visit her special bird in the animal hospital.

Evelyn had given the bird a name – Aurora, meaning "dawn". After two weeks in the medical incubator, Aurora was well enough to be moved to the rehabilitation aviary. She was always full of life, and had become very close to Evelyn. Every time Evelyn came to visit, she would flap her wings excitedly. She would also sing cutely to Evelyn. Aurora never failed to make Evelyn smile, no matter how frustrating the day's training had been. Evelyn enjoyed Aurora's company very much.

Heewon, who suffered horrific injuries to her arms and legs during Victor's attack on the nature reserve, was also recovering well. Determined to stand up to Victor, Heewon now practised martial arts harder than other first years, and she still volunteered in the Reptile House.

By the time Evelyn mastered that jump across the fire-breathing volcano in the computer world, it was already March. The weather was noticeably warmer and trees were growing back their leaves. Motivated by her recent success, Evelyn couldn't wait to start the next phase of her special training.

One particularly rainy and windy afternoon, Evelyn learned what was in store for her. Instead of practising martial arts outdoor, Guillermo decided they had better do something different indoor.

"We're going to the Knight Alley for some endurance training," he said.

Evelyn found herself back in the grand-looking cave where she had her nightmarish induction-camp encounters with spiders, centipedes and scorpions.

"What do I have to do this time?" she asked tensely.

"You'll see," Guillermo replied. He led her to one of the smaller caves and pulled the door open.

At first, it was all dark and Evelyn couldn't see a thing. Suddenly, the whole place lighted up in an eerie way: they were standing at the entrance to a narrow alley. On both sides of the alley were dozens of towering figures.

"Knights!" Guillermo described with boyish joy.

Evelyn walked up for a closer look. The knights were all made of iron, but had different body shapes and were clad in various styles of armours. Right now, all the knights were fast asleep, with their eyes shut.

Guillermo cleared his throat.

"This training is very straightforward. All you've got to do is concentrate on the exit and sprint towards it."

"Just make a dash for the exit?" Evelyn asked, disappointment in her voice. She was expecting something more challenging.

"Don't underestimate your enemies," said Guillermo, giving her a warning look, "these knights are fierce fighters! They will stop at nothing to make you fail –"

"How?" Evelyn interrupted, bored by the sleeping knights. Absent-mindedly, she extended her arm to the nearest knight, a particularly stout man, and tapped his shiny armour with her fingers. At once, the iron knight sprang to life. He opened his eyes, raised his sword and pointed it directly to Evelyn's heart.

"Whoa!" Evelyn yelled and jumped back in shock.

After that, there were a lot of scraping and banging: Evelyn had awoken the whole alley. The knights were stretching their limbs, brandishing their weapons – they were hostile, violent, ready to attack!

"There, I hope you understand what I mean," Guillermo concluded. "I'll go first. You'll come after me. All right?"

Evelyn nodded. "Got it."

Guillermo darted into the Knight Alley. What with his giant body and the knights lashing out at him vigorously, the narrow alley seemed even narrower. It wasn't an issue for Guillermo though. With perfect agility, he knelt and leapt to dodge the attacks – doubling back when necessary, sprinting forward when he had a chance. In less than a minute, he had already reached the other end of the alley. The exit door opened automatically – Guillermo stepped through, and was out of sight.

Now, it was Evelyn's turn.

She had barely set foot in the Knight Alley when the stout knight she touched earlier tried to head-butt her with his helmeted head. Evelyn dodged to one side just in time.

For a while, Evelyn's progress through the alley was quite slow, as all the dodging was very time-consuming. She thought it was a pity that the knights were made of iron; if only they were real, human knights, Evelyn could have hit back and forced her way through.

Twice, desperate to speed herself up, Evelyn decided she would just let the iron knights whack her with their iron parts … *Gosh.* It was so painful that she knew she had to be more careful.

Evelyn was about midway through the alley when she stumbled and almost fell flat on her face. A couple of knights had stuck out their feet and tried to trip her up with their iron boots. Evelyn frowned: that wasn't too knightly of them. Despite her anger, she forced herself to concentrate.

The exit, she reminded herself.

A few steps onward and Evelyn got whacked on the back of her head so hard she nearly blacked out. Feeling dizzy, she wheeled around … only to find herself face to face with a towering knight wielding a long iron club – she had been too distracted by the mean knights she didn't see it coming.

Enduring the throbbing headache that followed, Evelyn focused her mind on the exit and sprinted towards it with all her might!

Then, out of nowhere, an iron arm struck a bone-breaking blow across her ribs – the force of which caused pain to explode all over her metal core. Evelyn howled and crashed to the ground, tears streaming down her face.

When she looked up a few seconds later, Evelyn realised the knights had all gone out of line and swarmed towards her, ready to finish her off! Soon, they were hitting her with their arms or weapons – she couldn't tell which was which, as everything was made of iron.

Evelyn was so shocked she went numb. She was bleeding. She felt so lonely and helpless. *Where's Guillermo when I need him? Where's the emergency button?*

As if in answer to her questions, the floor suddenly opened up and Evelyn fell right through it: down and down she went, while the ferocious knights looked on from above, their bodies too large to get through the trapdoor.

There was a net at the bottom, breaking Evelyn's fall. She got entangled in the net, too weak to move her limbs.

"You tried to kill me!" Evelyn screamed at Guillermo as soon as she saw him.

Guillermo helped her out of the net and onto a chair. They were in a first-aid cave under the Knight Alley.

"How are you feeling?" he asked gently, pressing on her wounds to stop the bleeding.

"What do you care?" Evelyn yelled at him hysterically. "You almost killed me!"

"As a matter of fact, you wouldn't have fallen in the middle of the Knight Alley if you weren't so easily distracted," Guillermo reasoned, his tone calm and diagnostic – too calm, for Evelyn's liking.

Enraged, she stiffened up. "Are you blaming me now?"

"No, I'm not," he replied without hesitation. "Words cannot describe how sorry I am to see you injured." He avoided her glare as he spoke.

Evelyn let out a loud scoff. "This so-called endurance training is so dumb, useless and time-wasting. I never want to train again!"

"Everyone gets hit in the Knight Alley, it's really nothing to be ashamed of," said Guillermo, gazing at her with his bright blue eyes. "Evelyn, I understand how you feel."

"No, you don't!" she objected. "How could you? You are too gifted, too privileged. You succeed every time. You don't understand how it feels to fail."

Guillermo shook his head regrettably, but didn't argue. He made sure that all her wounds were properly dressed, and then gave her a tap on the shoulder.

"Evelyn, you need to come with me to Headmaster Mansion now."

Evelyn had no intention to move. "I want chocolate cakes!"

she demanded moodily.

"Of course you can have as many chocolate cakes as you want … after I've stitched up your wounds," Guillermo answered, his tone coaxing.

Tiredly, Evelyn stood up and followed Guillermo out of the cave.

CHAPTER 13

The Martial Arts Tournament

It had been a week since the incident in the Knight Alley. Evelyn was feeling so much better she was even ready to go back and try again. One afternoon, while walking across the lawn with 3D projections of kung fu masters demonstrating their signature moves, Evelyn noticed knots of students – mostly third years – surrounding one particular 3D projection. She darted forward for a closer look.

It wasn't a kung fu master at all, but a 3D notice. Bouncing at the top in shiny green were the words: 10th Martial Arts Tournament.

"So, are you joining?" Evelyn heard a third-year girl ask excitedly.

"Definitely!" a high-pitched, equally excited voice answered. "This is our shot at becoming the kung fu champion! And remember, it's our final year …"

Evelyn wasn't in her final year, nor did she dare to dream of becoming the kung fu champion. Still, she wanted to join – for a chance to challenge herself, if not for victory.

People were now jostling to sign up by shouting out their names. Evelyn was about to do the same when she noticed, in bright red letters:

"Eligibility: Final-year students may sign up directly. First and second-year students who wish to join must be recommended by teachers."

Evelyn's heart skipped a beat. *I have to seek Guillermo's approval before joining?*

The next day, Evelyn arrived at the training ground earlier than usual, her stomach full of butterflies. After her dreadful performance in the Knight Alley, she wondered what Guillermo would say about this. *Yes, or no?*

"Yes, Evelyn, go for it!" Guillermo's answer was quick and unreserved. "In fact, I do believe you can duel as well as a third year."

Evelyn stared at him, speechless. Guillermo rarely compared her to other students.

"You may even be better than a third year if you learn to use your strengths," he added, giving her a pat on the shoulder.

"You mean I actually have a chance to win?" Evelyn asked, surprised.

"Sure, why not?" He looked so earnest.

They were resting under a tree by the lake. Guillermo explained to Evelyn patiently: "Your weakness, obviously, is the lack of experience – you've only learned martial arts for a few months. It'll be hard for you to predict your opponents' moves."

Evelyn nodded. She was all ears.

"Your strengths are speed and power – use them well to compensate for your lack of experience. Surprise your opponents, hit them fast and hard right from the start!"

And that was exactly what Evelyn did. Guillermo's strategy worked out well for her. She fought match after match – some more difficult than others – and made it to the final. This was beyond her wildest dreams: *The way things are going, I may actually become the champion!*

Evelyn was congratulated by almost everyone she met. Even second and third-year students who she barely knew were wishing her good luck in the final.

Guillermo treated her to a big and hearty dinner at Headmaster Mansion.

"To victory," he said with a wide smile, raising his glass.

On the day of the grand final, Student Lodge was bustling with activity well before the starting time of the tournament. Evelyn found Heewon and Momoko in the kitchen, making banners. They had volunteered to cheer for Evelyn. There were lots of wires and bulbs on the table. The girls were trying to attach LED lights to the banners to make them sparkle.

Heewon stopped what she was doing when she saw Evelyn.

"Eat. You've got a big fight ahead of you," she said bossily.

Evelyn gave her a hug and sat down to eat. It was a big breakfast, with five meat dumplings, two fried eggs, a bowl of chicken noodles and a glass of orange juice.

"There's more orange juice in the fridge if you are thirsty."

"Thanks, I'd better not overeat today," Evelyn smiled at Heewon.

At that moment, Lily and Xiaojin burst into the kitchen.

"Almost missed wishing our special girl the very best of luck!" Lily said in a rush. "Evelyn, you've got to be careful of Joshua."

"That's right, we all saw him – he's fast and cunning," Xiaojin added, holding Evelyn's hand tightly, her brown eyes brimming with concern.

"I will be careful," Evelyn promised.

"Wish you all the best then," said Xiaojin, releasing Evelyn's hand.

"Evelyn, you've got to win!" Heewon cried out, waving a half-finished banner ardently.

"We've reserved the front rows to cheer for you," Momoko chimed in eagerly. "See you later!"

Evelyn said goodbye to her friends, then set off for the Arena of the grand final to get prepared for the tournament.

The Kung Fu Arena was built by the steep slope of one of the tallest mountains not far from campus. Looking up, Evelyn could see the magnificent peak, which was snow-capped all year round. But the Arena was situated some way down – it would have been surrounded by clouds on an average day, but luckily, today was very sunny, and the view was marvellous.

Evelyn could see the spectator stand clinging onto the steep slope of the mountain; and the floating stage, about the size of a football pitch, suspended in mid-air in front. She stopped for a moment to admire the mesmerising scenery. The whole place felt almost magical.

The Arena was so hard to reach there were cable cars to take people up the mountain. As Evelyn got off the cable car at the spectator stand, a student helper came to usher her into the competitor's designated changing room – a cave which ran all the way into the mountain.

The changing room was huge in size, and could easily fit in a team of ten. There were even sauna and massage beds. Evelyn was tempted to lie down and just relax …

Wake up, Evelyn! she chided herself. *This is battle time.*

It was getting noisier outside. Evelyn quickly changed into her fighting robe and came out to the waiting area. Her opponent, a muscular third-year student called Joshua, was already there. He acknowledged Evelyn with a curt nod, his face impassive.

The Arena, which only had a few spectators when Evelyn arrived, was now fully filled. The whole school was out there and in a wild mood. Students were chanting loudly, banging around, and brandishing all kinds of martial arts weapons.

Evelyn quickly checked the front rows. *There they are!* Heewon, Momoko, Lily and Xiaojin had brought other first years with them to cheer for Evelyn. They were waving colourful, flashing banners to show their support.

Next, Evelyn glanced at the teacher's seats, expecting to find Master Chow, Guillermo and the other teachers. She couldn't believe her eyes: there were so many guests! These people were anything but ordinary. They were dressed in awe-inspiring fighting robes or ethnic costumes, and most of them were strong, muscular, with ruddy complexion.

Evelyn was dumbstruck. *Wow.*

At that moment, fireworks were propelled into the sky, and the audience listened with rapt attention –

"Let the final, of the Tenth Martial Arts Tournament, officially begin," Master Chow declared in a booming voice.

The Arena exploded into deafening clapping.

Guillermo rose up to introduce the guests one by one. They were accomplished martial arts experts from around the world: the president of International Martial Arts Association, the head coach of Taekwondo Federation, a champion boxer from the US, a prestigious Shaolin monk … The more Evelyn listened, the more nervous she became – *I hope my fighting's good enough for them.*

Afterwards, there was a Chinese dragon dance performance at the spectator stand. The dragons were dancing along the aisles and allowing students to touch them. Evelyn had never seen a dragon dance before, and she thought it was pretty amazing.

As the dragon dance drew to a close, Evelyn and Joshua jogged through a corridor to get to another side of the mountain, where a helicopter stood waiting. They jumped in and shut the door.

The helicopter rose up, and in less than a minute, had positioned itself in the sky right above the floating stage. Evelyn could hear the commentator's voice, muted but unmistakeable:

"And now, let me present to you our two finalists –"

The pilot opened the helicopter door and threw out a thick rope.

"Evelyn will go first," he gestured to her, "and then you, Joshua."

Evelyn grabbed the rope, hopped out of the helicopter, and slid down to the stage. Out here, away from the cheering crowd, it was freezing cold. Evelyn looked down towards the stage: the referee was an African man – he had particularly broad shoulders, and was standing very straight. There was a doctor on standby just outside the fighting ring, and three security guards stationed at the outer perimeter of the stage.

As Evelyn's feet touched the stage, she could hear the commentator's excited voice reverberating from the spectator stand:

"Here comes … Evelyn Smith!"

Joshua landed twenty seconds after her, and Evelyn could hear the commentator calling out his name too.

The commentator went on to explain the rules. Evelyn

decided to stop listening to him: she had to focus on the present, on this stage, and on her opponent.

"Bow to each other!" the referee ordered.

They bowed. Evelyn met Joshua's eyes, expecting to see a beast – wild, fiery, ready to kill – like almost every opponent she met in the preliminaries. But Joshua was different. He was nothing like her average opponent. Instead, he looked calm, calculating, dangerously unpredictable …

"On the count of three," the referee shouted, holding out his arms to separate the two of them.

"One", "Two", "Three!"

Evelyn did her signature starting kick.

Joshua jumped away agilely, clearly anticipating her move.

It was a bit disappointing to miss her target, but Evelyn didn't give up. She followed up with a series of kicks and punches in quick succession, packing as much speed and power into them as she could.

These were not too effective either. Joshua was good at faking his moves, causing Evelyn to end up hitting the air numerous times. He also managed to find weak points on Evelyn to score for himself.

In the first couple of rounds, both Evelyn and Joshua were superbly cautious and defended well. As they entered further into the game, fatigue set in and both received more hits from one another – to the delight of an excited crowd, who shouted themselves hoarse every time one of them scored. As the scores for both Evelyn and Joshua were added up, the Arena became infinitely more rowdy.

It was the tightest match Evelyn had ever fought. After six hard-fought rounds, they arrived at the golden round – this time, whoever got a two-point lead would win, giving the other no chance to catch up.

Evelyn didn't know whether she was lucky or really a bit faster than Joshua, but she managed to score first with a kick to his head – a two-point target. And that was it: she won!

She felt a bit light-headed as Master Chow proclaimed in a deep and resonant voice:

"The champion of the Tenth Martial Arts Tournament is … Evelyn Smith!"

The spectators erupted into deafening cheers and applause. They were so loud that even far away on the floating stage, Evelyn could feel the warmth and joy radiating from the wild crowd. Evelyn bowed to the whole school and shook hands with Joshua. She was living out her dream: when victory finally came to her, it felt almost surreal.

Evelyn was bathing in her glory when she heard three loud bangs from the spectator stand. She frowned. *Those aren't firecrackers, are they?*

The "bang, bang, bang" went off again, this time accompanied by screams. Evelyn froze. There was no longer any doubt. These were gunshots!

In the spectator stand, students were cowering under their seats. A scuffle had broken out on the top rows – two gunmen had been caught on the spot by a group of brave third-year students. The gunmen were desperate to break free, but were restrained by those around them.

Afterwards, there were no more gunshots. Master Chow's powerful voice blared out over the loudspeakers.

"Evacuate now! Evacuate now!" He told the whole school. It was an order.

Students came out of their hiding places and flocked towards the exit at the back. Evelyn was relieved to see that her friends, despite seated in the front rows, managed to get to the exit as swiftly as everyone else.

At the teacher's stand, Master Chow, Guillermo and the visiting martial arts experts were all hurrying towards where the two gunmen were being held down.

A helicopter bearing the university name was fast approaching the floating stage, ready to whisk those on stage away. The helicopter was touching down at the stage when high-pitched warning sounds pierced the air.

Evelyn looked up and saw Aurora, her beloved bird, flying towards her and making the warning sounds. What Aurora came here for when everyone was trying to get out, Evelyn couldn't fathom.

The security guards on stage were now gesturing Evelyn to get into the helicopter. Evelyn ran on, closely followed by Joshua and the referee.

But Aurora was faster than them all. She started to attack the security guard nearest to the helicopter. *Which is strange,* thought Evelyn, as Aurora was a very gentle bird who rarely attacked anyone.

Evelyn sensed something was not quite right. It troubled her that Aurora was now pecking at all three security guards around the helicopter with irrepressible fury.

It was as Evelyn stepped onto the helicopter that everything dawned on her all at once. To her horror, she suddenly realised that the security guards around her were … fake! These were robots in disguise; she had been fooled by their human appearances and security guard uniforms. As for the university helicopter, it had probably been hijacked.

A wave of sheer panic swept across Evelyn. Screaming at the top of her voice, she tried to jump off the helicopter, but the security guards in the helicopter grabbed her from behind and swiftly took off.

"Come back!" Joshua shouted desperately, but there was not much he or the referee could do as the helicopter was rising too quickly.

The security guards went on to tie Evelyn up with heavy ropes to ensure she couldn't put up a fight. Just as Evelyn thought all was lost … that she was being flown to some unimaginable places to be tortured to death … her eyes fell upon the spectator stand.

An emergency bridge had been swung from the spectator stand to the floating stage. Master Chow and Guillermo were running across the bridge. Guillermo was wearing a pair of black goggles, and he was staring at the helicopter as he ran. It seemed obvious what he was trying to do – to bring back the university helicopter by remote control.

All of a sudden, the helicopter stopped rising and began to descend. It landed with a jolt! The next thing Evelyn knew, Master Chow and Guillermo were wrestling away the fake guards. Guillermo then jumped into the cockpit to untie her. Evelyn could see Guillermo talking to her, but she didn't hear a word: she was in shock. She couldn't believe she was almost abducted by some evil forces!

Evelyn didn't want to face the truth, but deep in her heart, she knew it was Victor: he had finally tracked her down. And from now on, he would be targeting her. *Heaven knows he won't stop until he finishes me off!*

Guillermo took Evelyn's elbow and gently led her out of the

helicopter. Evelyn could see that the fake security guards were being tied up by Joshua, the referee and the doctor. Master Chow was now poking at the robots with a fork-like device.

The doctor rushed to Evelyn as soon as he saw her.

"You're not going anywhere until I give you the all-clear!" he said rather self-righteously.

Guillermo waved the doctor away, assuring him that Evelyn was absolutely fine.

Of course, thought Evelyn glumly, *with so many robots caught red-handed today, the last thing anyone needs to know is that I have a metal core too.*

She followed Guillermo across the emergency bridge. As they set foot on the spectator stand, they were joined by Aurora, who clung to Evelyn's shoulder faithfully. Evelyn petted the bird and looked around …

This place, which had been bursting with life and joy merely half an hour ago, was now completely deserted – strewn across the seats and floor were personal belongings left behind by students in their hurry to get out of the Arena. Evelyn felt a chill in her spine. She was severely shaken by the fact that what should have been a brilliant day for the whole school could end up with so much horror … all because of Victor.

Guillermo took Evelyn back to Headmaster Mansion; Aurora flew away just before Evelyn entered. Evelyn was served three huge chocolate cakes straight from Guillermo's oven. The cakes were decadently sweet.

"How are you feeling?" Guillermo asked. He sat down and observed her warily.

"I'm good," Evelyn answered with her mouth full. She had been shell-shocked by what happened in the Kung Fu Arena, but Guillermo's cakes were so delicious they had somehow restored her spirit, and she was feeling much better now.

"What were those robots?" asked Evelyn. "Were they –" She hesitated, hoping against hope that she was wrong about Victor.

"Yes, they were Victor's," Guillermo's answer came back loud and clear. "Master Chow examined them. They had Victor's markings on them." Guillermo had been checking his smartglasses constantly for new messages.

"Where are the real security guards?" Evelyn asked with a grimace – this day must have been tough on them.

"Locked up, tied up, but miraculously unharmed," Guillermo replied.

"What about the gunmen and the fake security guards? Where are they now?"

Guillermo gave her a regretful look. "The robots will be handed over to the Chinese police after Master Chow has finished interrogating them."

"Oh." Evelyn muttered. Suddenly turning anxious, she said in a panicky voice, "What am I going to do now that Victor's after me? There are going to be more attacks, and he's going to get me … I mean, really soon!"

"Don't worry, I've got you covered," Guillermo told her calmly.

"How?" Evelyn exclaimed, her tone harsher than she intended. Guillermo clearly didn't understand: if he had got her covered, why was she almost abducted by Victor today?

"The flying armour will be ready to use in a couple of days," he explained. There was a hint of a smile on his lips.

"The what?"

"The flying armour. Would you like to see it for yourself, Evelyn?"

"Of course! Where is it?" Intrigued, Evelyn looked around the living room to see where the flying armour was hiding, but she couldn't find it.

Guillermo took her to the basement of Headmaster Mansion: it was a workshop. Near the entrance were plenty of wooden crates, metal boxes and some unfinished inventions. As they walked further into the underground chamber, Evelyn was amazed by all the high-tech gadgets around her.

At the heart of the workshop was a huge table, and on top of the table lay a single, magnificent suit. Mysterious green lights were shining upon it, apparently scanning for defects.

"A rocket suit!" Evelyn gasped in excitement. She had never seen anything like this – a suit with a rocket attached at the back.

"That's the flying armour, and it's in the final testing phase," said Guillermo seriously. "If all goes well – which is what I expect – you'll be able to fly in it in two days' time."

"I'll be able to fly in it?" Evelyn asked, her eyes wide.

"Yes. I designed the flying armour just for you, Evelyn, to enhance your fighting power," Guillermo answered warmly. "I'm sure it'll come in useful next time Victor tries to harm you."

Evelyn didn't know what to say. She felt so grateful and touched. Unbidden tears were welling up in her eyes. *Guillermo has designed and built a flying armour just for me!*

Guillermo chuckled and patted her shoulder.

"Flying lessons start on Monday. I'll meet you by the lake. Don't be late!"

CHAPTER 14

The Flying Armour

The annual Martial Arts Tournament was traditionally followed by the spring feast, where the champion would be honoured with a golden cup and, in the presence of the whole school, have her name inscribed on the Wall of Champions in the Great Hall.

All these would not be happening this year, because no one's in the mood to celebrate. In the eyes of the students, Victor's attack during the most important event of the school year meant he had declared war on the whole school. Students were outraged and wanted to fight back – it was just that they hadn't come up with a plan yet.

Evelyn was spared this uncertainty. She knew exactly what her next step was – to learn to fly!

On Monday morning, Evelyn set off towards the lake for her first flying lesson. She felt quite anxious, having never flown in a flying armour before. Along the way, Aurora hopped out of the bushes to join her. Evelyn brightened up and quickened her pace.

Guillermo was already by the lake. He was wearing a backpack, which looked ridiculously small on his enormous back, and his hands were free.

Wait, thought Evelyn, *where's the flying armour?*

Grinning at Evelyn's confused face, Guillermo took the flying armour out of his backpack, gave it a shake and held it against the morning sun.

Evelyn gasped. The flying armour seemed to have come alive: under the sun, the rocket part looked huge and powerful, while the silvery suit was skinny fit and looked very fashionable.

Mesmerized, Evelyn touched the suit with her fingertips … the material was soft and smooth, like silk.

"Try it on," said Guillermo, as he helped her slip into the flying armour.

Evelyn zipped herself up eagerly. She felt terrific! The flying armour was full of powerful features: a rocket at the back, weapon launchers on both arms, and a pair of smartglasses for control. It also fitted her perfectly, the silky suit felt like her own skin.

Filled with wonder, Evelyn put on the smartglasses to see what functions this suit had to offer.

"Try the flame button," Guillermo suggested. "Don't fire at me, of course," he added jokingly.

Evelyn quickly turned away from Guillermo to face the lake. She clicked "flame" on her smartglasses' screen using eye control.

Immediately, a ball of fire spat into the lake. It was an awesome sight. Evelyn decided to click the "flame" button continuously to see what would happen next.

From both her arms, streams of fire ejected simultaneously – bright, fiery, hot.

"Incredible!" Evelyn exclaimed, totally impressed.

There were also the "laser beam" and "bullet shooting"

functions, which sounded really exciting.

But Evelyn was distracted – standing out on the control screen was a flashing red button with a rocket symbol on it. Even the look of it was mighty and powerful. Tingling with curiosity, Evelyn pressed the flashing red button without hesitation.

"No!" shouted Guillermo.

It was too late. Evelyn had rocketed into the air. Up and up she went, until she lost balance in mid-air and began to somersault out of the sky – the rocket on her back firing uncontrollably in different directions as she somersaulted.

She fell back on the ground in a heap, knocked unconscious by the force.

When Evelyn opened her eyes again, she found herself lying in a patch of long grass. Her entire body was sore and aching. She looked up and saw Guillermo flying towards her on a hoverboard.

He landed right next to her.

"Are you okay?" he asked. His voice was filled with concern, and his face was almost touching hers.

Evelyn didn't answer. She moaned and tried to sit up on her own.

Guillermo held out his muscular arm to her, but Evelyn didn't take it.

"Are you okay?" he repeated, frowning.

Evelyn pouted. "Yes," she replied curtly.

"Then let's try again," said Guillermo. "This time, I'm going to teach you how to fly properly –"

"I don't want to do this today!" Evelyn interrupted him ill-temperedly.

Guillermo stared at her, surprised, and then shrugged. "In this case, let's try again tomorrow. You know, Evelyn, we're running out of time."

"I don't care about anything right now!" she screamed and looked away.

Guillermo spent the rest of the lesson teaching Evelyn to duel. It was hard and intense enough for her to let off steam. Afterwards, she felt a lot better and was ready to fly again.

The next day, Guillermo flew to their meeting place on his hoverboard. Seeing that Evelyn had already put on her flying armour, he hovered in mid-air and gestured her to come with him.

"It's easier to use voice control," he advised.

"Rise towards Guillermo!" Evelyn shouted at her suit, probably too loudly.

The flying armour rocketed her into the sky, going far above and beyond where Guillermo was. Then, with a violent jerk, it dropped her out of the sky.

Evelyn was scared, but forced herself to keep still – she didn't want to lose balance again.

When the flying armour finally stabilised, Evelyn looked to her left and found that it had just brought her shoulder to shoulder with Guillermo. She opened her mouth in disbelief: *Wow, that's precise.*

"I'm glad you didn't panic." Guillermo gazed at her fondly and gave her a pat on the back. "See, Evelyn, you can do it! Let's get back to the ground."

Standing agilely on his hoverboard, Guillermo soared over some trees and glided smoothly onto a piece of grassland.

Evelyn followed him clumsily, telling her suit to "go

straight", "watch out for the trees", "land on the grass now", and "don't crash into Guillermo!"

She toppled awkwardly next to Guillermo's hoverboard, but got back on her feet really quickly.

"Whoo-hoo!" Evelyn punched the air and let out a whoop of victory.

Guillermo rolled his eyes at her but said nothing.

They sat side by side on the grass. Guillermo threw Evelyn a chocolate bar and munched on a protein bar himself. He explained to her, "Flying is not something you can learn by reading the manual –"

A sharp cry pierced the peaceful air. They both looked up: Aurora was flying speedily across the sky to join them. She landed on Evelyn's shoulder in a calm yet alert manner.

"Flying is about experience," Guillermo continued, "you really need to go out, fly your thing, and get the know-how."

"Great. I'm ready … ready for anything!" Evelyn said wildly.

They rose into the sky together, flying abreast – Evelyn in her flying armour, Guillermo on his hoverboard. Guillermo grinned and signalled "catch me" as he sped forward and soared over a series of mountains.

Evelyn was falling behind. She uttered her commands … and SWOOSH! The flying armour rocketed her over the mountain ranges towards Guillermo. They high-fived each other.

Looking down at a gorgeous waterfall now, Evelyn hesitated as Guillermo dived fearlessly at the waterfall, then soared back into the sky with a triumphant roar.

Adrenaline spiking through her body, Evelyn dived, almost crashing into the pool below the waterfall, but changed course just in time … *Hooray!* She rocketed into the air magnificently.

Guillermo led Evelyn into an area of low-hanging clouds – sometimes she could see him, sometimes she couldn't – it was like playing hide-and-seek. He suddenly turned around and shouted, "It's my turn to catch you, Evelyn!"

Eager to avoid being caught, she stopped talking to her suit and switched back to eye control using the smartglasses' screen. Guillermo's hoverboard was no match for the rocket power of Evelyn's flying armour, and she managed to outfly him every time he chased after her.

It was such a wild and carefree world up here – there were just the two of them. Evelyn laughed loudly and freely. She was still laughing as they returned to the ground after spending half a day chasing each other in the clouds.

Over the next two weeks, Evelyn flew out with Guillermo frequently, practising her flying skills around some of the tallest mountains near the university.

After one truly pleasant morning session, they were about to turn back when Evelyn saw smoke billowing out of a hidden cave. The cave was halfway up a mist-shrouded mountain and extremely difficult to spot because of the thick mist hanging around.

Evelyn immediately pointed the suspicious cave to Guillermo. He nodded, and together, they dived … landing on a small but dense patch of bushes near the cave's entrance.

Now that she was close enough, Evelyn could feel something ominously familiar about this cave. She remembered reading about similar structures in the news: caves which were always hidden deep inside mountains, and rapidly springing up across the world … If her thinking was correct, this could actually be a Victor's robot lair! There had already been a few discoveries in America and Europe. *But in China?* This could probably be the first sighting.

Guillermo was now creeping forward through the thick bushes for a better look at the entrance – carrying his hoverboard in one hand, and holding out his smartglasses in the other. Evelyn followed closely. She peeped at Guillermo's smartglasses' screen and saw several programs running simultaneously. He was pinpointing their GPS location, snapping photos of the cave, detecting abnormal heat fluctuation, and analysing unnatural sound waves.

Stealthily, Evelyn looked out: two men with guns were guarding the cave entrance. Having been fooled once, Evelyn immediately checked … and sure enough, they were actually robots, with human appearance.

As Evelyn watched, two more robots emerged. They were each pushing a truckload of scrap metal, which they unloaded into a pit next to the cave. These robots probably worked inside, as they were made of metal and not covered in human skin.

Evelyn could see that the cave was well-defended. Apart from the two gun-wielding guards, there was a huge cannon sitting at the mouth of the cave. Hanging from the ceiling of the cave entrance were cameras, sensors and other surveillance devices. There was a piece of open land in front of the cave, which was surprisingly empty, and Evelyn had an uncanny feeling that it was a trap.

Something is definitely going on here, something evil, she thought, grinding her teeth.

Browsing through the manual of her flying armour, Evelyn's eyes fell upon the "high-tech scanning" function. She clicked "run program" via eye control, and then waited. *Is it going to be a revelation, or a disappointment?*

The scanning revealed an astonishingly complex structure inside the cave. There were many levels, and elevators to provide access to each level. Hundreds of robots were currently at work inside: polishing swords, making guns, building cannons and packing explosives.

Evelyn was so intrigued she moved past Guillermo and edged closer and closer towards the open land in front of the cave entrance, eager to scan deeper into the robot lair …

BOOM! Something exploded near her feet. Evelyn was blown backward into the air, landing painfully on some shattered rocks. In front of her, the ground had been blasted open, leaving a huge crater which was several metres deep.

I should have been more careful, she thought regretfully. *Where's Guillermo?*

He was nowhere to be seen.

Evelyn broke out in a cold sweat and started to shake. She feared she might have killed Guillermo by accidentally triggering the explosion. She was going to call out his name when rocks and debris rained down around her, and BOOM!

A second blast went off – this one was so much louder than the first.

Evelyn was temporarily turned deaf. When her hearing returned a few seconds later, she could hear robots running in her direction: the distinctive sound of metal feet against compact soil was bloodcurdling. She couldn't see them in the smoke and dust, but judging from the sound, Victor's robots seemed to be closing in on her really quickly.

Gripped by fear that someone was going to shoot her, Evelyn rocketed into the air for dear life. She rose and rose, penetrating thick layers of suspending dust and low clouds, until finally she reached the clear blue sky. Even then Evelyn dared not let her guard down: she changed direction and flew across the sky, just to make sure no Victor's robot was on her tail.

When Evelyn finally slowed down thinking she had successfully shaken off all her enemies, she was appalled to sense something flying towards her at high speed –

It was Guillermo, speeding towards her on his hoverboard.

Evelyn instantly relaxed.

"We're alive!" she yelled ecstatically, somersaulting skilfully in the sky using her flying armour.

Guillermo hovered beside Evelyn, pleased to see her but also looking cautious. He parted his lips slightly, as if he wanted to scold her … for not rocketing into the sky immediately after the first explosion, and thus putting herself in danger. Next moment, he pressed his lips firmly together and simply gave her a little smile.

He didn't want to spoil her moment of grand escape.

CHAPTER 15

Virtual Reality Fighting

Evelyn's joy of escape didn't last long. Flying back to campus with Guillermo, she began to worry about whether Victor's robots had seen her; and if so, did they recognise her? One thing was certain – now that she had awoken an entire army of Victor's robots, there would be another attack very soon.

Evelyn felt overwhelmed. She had seen the dangerous weapons Victor's robots were making. This was urgent: *My friends … the whole school … people need to know what's coming!*

Evelyn decided to be frank with Guillermo. As they landed together, she told him she was chased by robots from the mountain lair. Moving closer to his muscular body, she shared with him her fears and worries.

Guillermo listened carefully. He nodded and patted her shoulder.

"Don't worry, Evelyn. We're prepared." He sounded calm and composed.

"All right … how?" she muttered uncertainly.

"Remember the VR computer lab that I showed you?" he asked, brimming with confidence.

"Yes I do, the virtual reality computer lab!" Evelyn cried out, feeling hopeful. And then, remembering how that place was far from completed last time she visited it, she added, "When will it be ready?"

"Today," Guillermo answered with a twinkle in his eyes. "In fact, I'm on my way to meet Master Chow for the final testing. If you would like to come with me, Evelyn –"

"Of course!" she shouted eagerly.

They walked to the site of the VR computer lab. Guillermo pushed away some fallen branches to reveal a trapdoor on the ground.

"This is a shortcut for Master Chow and myself," he explained.

"Interesting," said Evelyn, impressed by how well-concealed it was.

Climbing down, they arrived at an underground chamber. There was an elevator inside. They got into the elevator, which dropped down at breakneck speed, until suddenly, it jolted to a halt.

"The war rooms," announced a fruity female voice.

It was very quiet down here. The corridor was illuminated by warm white lights, and lingering in the air was a heavy smell of leather. Walking through the corridor, Evelyn could see conference facilities and simple living quarters. She peered into one of the rooms, her eyes widening with wonder as she came face-to-face with a dozen brand-new, very comfortable-looking gaming chairs. *That's where the leather smell comes from!*

"The war rooms are part of the VR computer lab specially designed for those of us who are leading the fight to work closely together," said Guillermo with passion. "And these chairs you are looking at are link units – they allow us to go and fight in the computer world together. There are more link units in the main hall of the VR computer lab."

At that moment, Master Chow appeared. He smiled at them and got down to business.

"Let's begin our final testing," he said, jumping into one of the link units without delay. He invited Evelyn to the unit on his right.

Evelyn jumped in enthusiastically: the chair was so bouncy and could even be reclined into a bed! She felt honoured to be sitting here, alongside Master Chow and Guillermo, doing the final testing …

"When I count to three, you'll press the gold button," Master Chow commanded in an authoritative voice.

The three of them landed in the computer simulated world together. It was a desert setting. The sand was drearily orange and there were a few cactuses in the horizons. Above them, the sun was sweltering. Evelyn looked at herself – she was exactly like her real-world self, down to the scarf and jacket she was wearing.

They took a long stroll in the desert, duelled on the sand repeatedly, and fired all sorts of weapons. By the time Master Chow gave them the thumbs up, which signalled "the end", the sun was already setting in the computer world. Evelyn quickly pressed the gold button in her pocket –

She was back in the comfortable chair of the link unit.

After the success of the final testing, Master Chow announced to the whole school that an opening ceremony would be held that very afternoon.

Evelyn went back to Student Lodge to meet up with her

friends. The girls were thrilled.

"We're about to get our first glimpse of … ta-da … the VR Computer Lab!" Momoko exclaimed dramatically, as though this was some fancy place out of a fairy tale.

"Afternoon classes cancelled to make way for an opening ceremony? Surely, this must be something serious," said Xiaojin sensibly.

Lily's eyes were alight with curiosity. "I wonder what they have built this time …"

"I hope our kung fu training will come in useful," Heewon chimed in, always so keen to fight.

They set off excitedly, chatting along the way. It was a very invigorating walk through the dense forest. Before long, they arrived at the main entrance to the VR computer lab – an elevator lobby built into a mountain cave at the side of the lake.

"This is cool," said Momoko, glancing at the wilderness around them. "The whole thing seems to be underground."

"It's actually under the lake," said Evelyn, holding Momoko's arm.

"Even better!" Momoko chortled.

The five of them entered a glass elevator together. As the elevator descended through the cave, they could see stalagmites and stalactites all around them. Lights – green, purple, orange – were shone upon the strange-looking rocks to create a mystical atmosphere. The beauty was beyond words, and all they could say was … "Wow!"

The elevator stopped at the base of the cave. Afterwards, they had to walk through a short tunnel, which led to the main hall of the VR computer lab.

"Unbelievable!" cried Heewon, wide-eyed.

The main hall of the VR computer lab was a huge, state-of-the-art chamber under the lake and looked like a space mission control room. Arranged in circle after circle around the grand centre stage were a hundred and fifty link units – most of which already occupied by students who arrived early. Evelyn and her friends quickly found seats for themselves.

Stretching out in their link units, they could see the glass ceiling clearly, and rays of sunlight which were shining down from above. Penetrating the lake water and ceiling glass, these rays were then refracted into the VR computer lab as rippling bluish lights, creating a very otherworldly atmosphere that felt far removed from Earth and reality.

If anyone had been looking forward to a relaxing opening ceremony, now they knew: this was about something much more serious, even sinister … because why else would the university need to build such a sophisticated, cutting-edge VR computer lab?

Master Chow rose up from the centre stage. The stage rotated slowly, allowing him to face the entire audience, one angle at a time.

"Some of you may be wondering what a VR computer lab has to do in a martial arts university," he began solemnly.

The whole chamber fell silent – a few students nodded.

"Let me be honest with you. We are gathered here today because a need has arisen: the need to fight Victor."

There was a collective gasp at the mention of Victor. Then, in a gesture of solidarity, students joined hands. From those standing at the back to those sitting in link units in front, the message couldn't be clearer – the whole school was in this together.

Evelyn shook Xiaojin's arm on her right, giving her a

mischievous wink. Xiaojin winked back, and pulled a glum face.

"As we all know, Victor has escalated his attacks in recent months. Our school, together with our neighbour the nature reserve, have already been attacked twice. Around the globe, similar events are happening. Most places are less lucky than us: people have suffered and died."

The atmosphere in the VR computer lab grew tense and heavy. Students, still holding each other's hands, stared at Master Chow. Their faces spoke of passion, fury, and above all, an eagerness to fight evil.

"When Victor spreads fire in our world, we have to douse it; when his accomplices shoot people, we need to catch them. But ultimately, we all know that Victor is a 'shapeless evil'. To terminate him, we need to get into the computer world –"

Students glanced at each other. There was this "Oh I see!" moment as dawning comprehension gripped the under-lake chamber.

"That's where our VR computer lab fits in," Master Chow concluded in an inspirational tone. "Ladies and gentlemen, if you would like to fight Victor with me, this is your chance. Go to the intranet and sign up for the VR fighting programme. Training may start immediately, or at your convenience. Time is running out, so do hurry!"

A murmur of thrilled interest rose from the students.

"And now, let's move on to our opening ceremony!"

Guillermo led a group of teachers onto the centre stage. There was a ribbon cutting ceremony. The moment they cut the ribbon, confetti shot out of the walls and sparkling strips of paper rained down the entire VR computer lab. A dragon dance performance quickly followed. The Chinese dragons paraded around students, just like they did on the spectator stand in the Martial Arts Tournament, and the whole school went wild with excitement.

Tea was served afterwards, which Evelyn and her friends skipped; they had decided to sign up and train right away. While Evelyn waited for the link unit to start up, she saw Master Chow, Guillermo and a few teachers retreating into the war rooms. Her eyes followed them till they disappeared behind closed doors.

Evelyn and her friends trained throughout the afternoon and deep into the evening. Afterwards, they walked back to Student Lodge together.

"Well, if this is how we're going to fight Victor, I'm not sure I'll be of much use," Lily sighed. "I can't believe I 'died' so many times. Unlike you, Evelyn, you didn't even scratch yourself!"

"That's because I've tried those tasks before," Evelyn spoke honestly. Their first training turned out to be the same "tropical island" program Guillermo led Evelyn into some time ago, so of course, she did exceptionally well.

She hugged her friends goodnight and went back to her room.

Gazing into the cloudy, starless night sky as she lay in bed to rest, Evelyn was suddenly overcome by ominous feelings: *Guillermo said we are prepared for Victor's attack because of the VR computer lab. And yet, my friends ... Lily, Xiaojin, Momoko, Heewon ... and probably other students too ... they are clearly not prepared to fight anytime soon.*

Evelyn shuddered as she recalled the army of Victor's robots hiding in their multi-level cave deep inside the mountain, and those awful weapons they were making, packing, ready to unleash – she felt quite certain some of the explosives were destined for their university.

Evelyn tried to stay awake and keep watch: she wanted to be the first person to know and alert the whole school when Victor's robots came marching down the university. But the long day took its toll on her. She yawned, rolled over, and slipped into sleep mode in spite of herself.

In the middle of the night, Evelyn was woken up by a loud explosion. The whole building shook; the vibration resonated through her metal core. Looking up, she saw red laser beaming into her room – her wardrobe was on fire!

The sirens began to wail, penetrating the walls of Student Lodge with such eardrum-piercing, heart-wrenching sounds it felt as if doomsday had arrived.

"Victor's going to kill us all," Evelyn mumbled darkly to herself.

She swung her legs off the bed, burst out of her room and dashed through the corridor. Along the way, Evelyn activated her high-tech infrared eyes, scanning through three floors as she ran – hers, above, below – just to make sure no one was left behind. She could see that other rooms had caught fire too. *Well, at least everyone has got out.*

As Evelyn reached the stairs, a second explosion rocked the building. She could feel sonic waves travelling through the walls, followed by sounds of glass shattering. The lights at the stairs went out. It was so oppressively dark. Evelyn's senses sharpened: she heard a girl next to her stifling a scream, and others cursing Victor under their breath. The emergency lighting kicked in soon after. The stairs became dimly-lit. Evelyn quickly made her way down alongside other students.

The ground floor smelt burnt and was covered in water – apparently, it had caught fire and triggered the sprinkler system. They walked across the flooded lobby to get out of the building.

Stepping outside, Evelyn took a deep breath and looked back, dreading what she might see …

Student Lodge was a smouldering mess: the outer walls were badly charred, a lot of windows were shattered, and part of the roof had collapsed. Evelyn's stomach lurched when she saw up to twelve Victor's robots marching downhill towards town. Some of them were breathing fire, while others were firing laser and sonic weapons like maniacs. They were burning down trees and destroying buildings as they went, causing a trail of destruction.

A large group of students had already gathered at the assembly point. Evelyn climbed up a rock to look for her friends. *There they are!* She quickly jumped back to the ground and wove her way through the crowd. She gave each of her friends a tight, warm hug.

"Can't believe this is happening," Momoko uttered, resting her head on Evelyn's shoulder.

"At least we're alive, which is what matters most," said Evelyn, wrapping her arms around Momoko to comfort her.

Lily and Heewon's grim faces mirrored the sombre mood of the night: Student Lodge had been brutally attacked, and yet the attackers were on the run …

Around them, students were snapping photos, eager to tell the whole world what Victor just did. Some students were in tears. Many were talking on their phones telling family and friends not to worry. A few angry young men tried to chase after Victor's robots, but were restrained by their peers. Evelyn also saw a team of third years trying to extinguish wildfires left behind by Victor's robots – they didn't seem too successful.

Momoko had cut herself while running down the stairs, so Evelyn went to the first-aid tent with her to get some sterile dressings. When they came out of the tent, they found the sky being lighted up spectacularly. Everybody was looking above: several high-tech drones from the nearby fire station – flying in formation – had come to tackle the remaining flames on campus by showering blue fluorescent powder.

It was a very impressive sight. Evelyn and Momoko leaned on fences to watch the firefighting drones. Then, out of the corner of her eye, Evelyn saw Guillermo and two other teachers running on the path below. Guillermo's face was hard and unsmiling. He seemed to be giving orders to the other teachers.

Evelyn looked away. Barely a minute later, she felt a hand on her shoulder –

"Here you are! I've been worried about you," Guillermo said warmly, a look of relief on his face.

Evelyn felt as though a current had just run through her. *Has he been looking for me in particular?*

"I'm fine," she answered, flushing.

"Good to hear that," said Guillermo, giving her an affectionate pat on the shoulder before turning his attention to other students.

Evelyn realised Momoko had been staring at her.

"Wow. The headmaster does care about you," she said with admiration.

Evelyn blushed.

"Guillermo's the kind of teacher who likes to make sure his students are all right," she explained, smiling shyly.

After the attack, Student Lodge was sealed off. The whole school spent the rest of the night in the sports centre. Sleeping bags were provided, but no one was in the mood to sleep. Everyone was eager to stay up-to-date with Victor's latest attacks: places he targeted, damages he caused, number of deaths and injuries he was responsible for …

Unfortunately, their Internet access was cut off shortly after they settled in the sports centre. For a moment, the sports hall erupted into loud curses and angry shouts.

An announcement was made: The school had just contacted the wireless network provider. Due to damages to underground cables, there would be no connection until further notice.

It was a restless night. By dawn, someone suddenly shouted: "The Internet's back on!" There was a buzz of excitement as everyone hurried to get back online. This was followed by an eerie silence as the heart-stopping news sank in: overnight, simultaneous Victor's attacks had been reported around the globe. The attack on their university was bad enough, but the situation at Chengdu City below them was worse, and so were the situations in several other countries.

In a series of pictures uploaded by Chengdu residents, Evelyn could see high-tech drones hovering above the city fighting the various blazes left behind by Victor's robots. The Chinese army could be seen patrolling the main streets with their armoured vehicles.

There was another news feed from the US which showed an entire village being burnt down by Victor's robots – up to a hundred people were reported missing and feared dead …

Evelyn gritted her teeth, disgusted with Victor's brutality.

He must be stopped at all costs, she thought furiously, *I'm going to stop him!*

CHAPTER 16

Legend of the Sacred Eagle

That morning, an announcement was made to the whole school: In view of the latest emergency situation, all classes would be suspended with immediate effect.

Students flooded into the VR computer lab to continue their computer world training. Their fighting spirit was higher than ever – they vowed to kill Victor in the computer world … once and for all!

Meanwhile, Evelyn received a message from Guillermo, summoning her to Master Chow's office. "There's something we need to discuss with you," he wrote, but didn't explain further.

What will that be? thought Evelyn, as she hurried up the hill towards Master Chow's stone house at the edge of the cliff.

When she arrived, Evelyn observed that Master Chow's office looked different: the wooden furniture had been removed, and projectors had been brought in and placed along the walls.

A holographic conference was about to start. Master Chow was standing in the middle of the room, ready to greet their guest. Guillermo was standing beside the projectors and out of the spotlight; he waved at Evelyn to join him.

Standing beside Guillermo now, Evelyn was eager to see

who their special guest was –

Pop! A holographic person materialised in front of them. He had a transparent body which was glowing in bright orange.

At first, Evelyn felt excited. She froze when she realised who she was looking at. *Good heavens, it's Ronald!* Evelyn hadn't seen him for a long time. Mixed feelings about this man threatened to overwhelm her.

All right, he was her creator, a really intelligent scientist; and yet, he was also a man who was totally insensitive to her feelings, who thought it was funny to let her wake up as a bodiless head; and worst of all, he was a robot killer, which was why she had to run away from him in the first place.

Evelyn clearly remembered their last moment together: Ronald tried to activate her special firing system to kill other robots. He was enraged when she refused. And since then, she had been living in the fear that he would terminate her in revenge – at the slightest excuse, if an excuse was needed at all.

This man is not to be trusted! thought Evelyn, feeling emotional.

"How are things looking on your side?" Ronald asked Master Chow.

"Grim," Chow sighed. "We've got a Victor lair in the mountains. The robots came out last night and wreaked havoc on campus, spreading fire from my school all the way down to Chengdu City."

"I'm sorry," Ronald replied sincerely. After a moment's silence, he asked, "Where's Evelyn? You said she would be here."

Master Chow gestured Evelyn to come up to him.

"Hi, Ronald," she said awkwardly.

"Nice to see you, Evelyn!" Ronald greeted her with genuine

delight. "Where's the headmaster?"

"He's – er –" Evelyn mumbled.

"I'm right here," Guillermo jumped forward and answered with a burst of energy.

"Good." Ronald nodded approvingly. "I'm glad you keep your promise, young man – I see my girl's still in one piece."

He returned his attention to Evelyn.

"How's your kung fu training going, Evelyn? Are you more disciplined now?"

"I'm doing fine –"

"She's doing great," Guillermo interjected enthusiastically, "so much better than when I first met her."

Ronald glanced at the two of them in a strange way, but didn't question further.

He turned to Master Chow.

"Let's get to the point. I'm going to show you some of the weapons my team and I have designed to fight Victor in the computer world."

Holographic models of the weapons immediately shot out of the projectors in quick succession – sparkling purple and transparent, they now hovered in mid-air in Master Chow's office. They were an amazing collection: rifles with infinite bullets, a sword pulsing with electricity, a hammer that was light enough to hold yet hit with the weight of a mountain … *Wow.*

Evelyn was feeling overwhelmed when Ronald asked suddenly, "Evelyn, what's your personal weapon in the computer world?"

"My what?" she blurted out, tearing her eyes away from the fascinating models.

"Your personal weapon," Ronald repeated.

She shook her head, looking pitifully clueless.

"A personal weapon, Evelyn, is something that resonates with your heart … something that can significantly enhance your fighting power in the computer world," Ronald explained.

"I see."

"To become a great fighter in the computer world, you've got to find your personal weapon," Ronald continued passionately. "My team has designed weapons to suit every taste. Look carefully and see if there's something that calls out to you personally."

Evelyn took a step forward and gazed at the purple weapons hovering around Master Chow's office. Powerful though they were, none of them felt right to her heart, and she told Ronald so.

Ronald wasn't offended; quite the contrary, he seemed very understanding.

"You've got to keep finding, Evelyn. With the right personal weapon, you'll be able to unleash your greatest fighting power," he encouraged her. "Victor's growing stronger by the day. We need you. The world needs you."

"Don't worry, we'll guide her along the way," Master Chow chimed in, his tone reassuring.

"Be warned, she could be a tricky case," Ronald added. "Let her choose, and don't rush her into things."

"You have my word," Master Chow promised.

After the holographic conference was over, Evelyn followed Guillermo to the university's main gate where a group of students were hugging each other emotionally. International students were given the option to be escorted to Chengdu International Airport after Victor's latest attacks, but almost everyone chose to stay and stand with the school.

There were tearful goodbyes at the school gate as those students who had to leave were surrounded by their friends. One girl looked particularly grief-stricken – her eyes were so red she had clearly been crying a lot. Evelyn overheard that her home town in the US had been hit, and her parents were injured. It was with much reluctance that she decided to go home and be strong for her family, while her friends stayed on to fight Victor.

The departing students were escorted to two police vans. It was quite a scene: in front of the police vans were motorcycles leading the way, and at the back were two armoured vehicles with soldiers on standby.

The sergeant in charge came up to introduce himself in English. He then opened the doors of the police vans to welcome students on board. Guillermo swiftly walked up to thank him. Evelyn heard the sergeant say, "Don't worry, headmaster, your students are in good hands."

The sergeant then jumped onto one of the leading motorcycles. With lights flashing, the motorcade left the university and made its way towards the airport.

That afternoon, Evelyn was summoned again – this time to the war rooms within the VR computer lab. She entered to find Guillermo and Master Chow deep in conversation. A series of 3D images were projected into the room, including scans taken by Evelyn and Guillermo the day before, and those taken by drones thereafter.

Guillermo immediately beckoned Evelyn over to stand beside him. Master Chow nodded at Evelyn and continued, "These before and after images show that since yesterday, there has been a rapid increase in robot numbers in Victor's lair near our school." Pointing to an image which showed a particularly crowded cave, he added darkly, "Apparently, they are not just churning out weapons, but also robots. New robots are being made as we speak."

He changed to another set of projections.

"These CCTV images captured in the nature reserve show that the robots are actively exploring the areas around us, ready for another attack – anytime – at Victor's command."

Evelyn shuddered: she wished Victor's army wasn't going to advance too quickly. *For heaven's sake, our school has just survived one big attack!*

"We can't wait," Master Chow concluded. "First thing tomorrow morning, we're going out with the local people. We're going to search the mountains and destroy any Victor's robot we see."

"How do we know they are Victor's robots, and not some benign robots passing by?" asked Evelyn abruptly. "Or maybe they are here to hunt Victor's robots too."

"Unbeknown to us?" said Master Chow, peering over his smartglasses at Evelyn. "No, that's impossible."

Evelyn took a moment to think about it … "All right, sorry to interrupt."

"After the robots in the area have been cleared," Master Chow went on, "everyone's going back to the VR computer lab. We're going to find and kill Victor in the computer world."

"Where will we find him?" asked Evelyn.

"I've identified a few places that Victor could be hiding in, so that's not a problem."

"But my personal weapon," Evelyn exclaimed, getting anxious. "Where can I find it? Surely I need one to fight Victor!"

Master Chow sighed. "You heard Ronald, Evelyn. Things

like that can't be rushed. When the time comes, you'll know."

"Really?" Evelyn muttered, feeling lost. *To defeat Victor, I need to be at my best … Ronald said a personal weapon can unleash my greatest fighting power …*

"Come on, let's go," said Guillermo, taking her hand.

Evelyn followed Guillermo out of the VR computer lab, her mind in turmoil. They walked a short way through the forest and arrived at a large, grassy clearing. In front of them was a black helicopter. Its turbine engines started to roar as soon as they approached.

Evelyn brightened up. The last time she sat side-by-side with Guillermo in a plane, they were on the journey from London to Sichuan, China. The memories brought a smile to Evelyn's lips … *Those good old times!*

"Are you taking me to meet someone?" Evelyn asked, still smiling.

"Actually, I figure you might want a break after all that have happened," Guillermo answered, watching Evelyn's reactions closely. "So, we're flying over the nature reserve, just for fun."

"Let's do this!" Evelyn bellowed, punching the air excitedly.

The helicopter lifted off smoothly. Flying across the sky, Evelyn could see the extensive damage Victor's robots did to the nature reserve: large patches of forest had been burnt down, which would take years to recover.

A Buddhist temple had its top blasted off, exposing the interior –

"What's that?" asked Evelyn, pointing to an enormous set of skeleton poking out of the temple – it looked like the skeleton of a giant eagle.

"That's the Temple of the Sacred Eagle," came Guillermo's

voice.

"Are the bones real?" she asked curiously.

"So they say," Guillermo answered, his tone dismissive. "In this part of Sichuan, there are dragon and unicorn bones that people claim are real too."

"What's the story about this sacred eagle?"

"Legend has it that during the time of Three Kingdoms, a female warrior rescued the sacred eagle from Mount Emei – one of the four sacred mountains in China. The eagle and the warrior fought together and won many battles. The warrior even rode on the eagle to travel to hell, and successfully saved the world from doom," Guillermo narrated fluently.

"You do know a lot about Chinese folklore," Evelyn praised, truly impressed.

"If you had lived here long enough, you would have heard the stories too."

Evelyn stared at the skeleton of the sacred eagle, mesmerised. For some inexplicable reason, it reminded her of Aurora ... *But Aurora is small, nothing like this huge eagle* ... Evelyn forced herself to stop obsessing over such a ludicrous idea.

After the helicopter ride, Evelyn went to the IT Centre to continue her computer world training. She met Aurora along the way, who clung on to Evelyn's shoulder and refused to leave – Aurora's expressive eyes spoke clearly of how she would love to be pampered. Evelyn decided to take the bird with her.

They entered one of the private rooms together. Evelyn put Aurora on her lap and got to work. She chose the "Forest Challenge" program in the drop-down menu, loaded it and pressed the green button.

At once, she found herself in a dense forest. A storm was

raging, and rain was pouring down so intensely it was hard to see anything beyond the nearest trees.

Evelyn wasn't afraid. She was thrilled: she ran on and on in the forest. As she arrived at a clearing, Evelyn noticed an enormous bird hovering above her, as if guarding her …

Evelyn looked up and couldn't believe her eyes: it was her beloved Aurora! Basically Aurora still looked like herself, except that she had grown so big and gorgeous – Aurora had somehow transformed into a truly magnificent beast of the sky!

Filled with joy and excitement, Evelyn called out to Aurora. The giant bird flapped her mighty wings and landed next to Evelyn. Evelyn carefully slid her leg over Aurora's back, and Aurora took off like a shot!

"Whoo-hoo!" Evelyn yelled wildly. They flew over high mountains and in deep valleys. Evelyn could feel Aurora's power – it was a miraculous and otherworldly feeling.

Back in their room in the IT Centre, Evelyn discovered Aurora's little secret. Apparently, Aurora had flown into an advanced brainwave scanning machine in the room and activated it, landing herself in the computer world.

Not much had changed about Aurora though: she was still a small, cute bird. At this moment, she was hopping hyperactively next to Evelyn's fingers, asking to be caressed.

Evelyn couldn't wait to tell Guillermo about Aurora's special power. After all, it was Guillermo who signed the paper to let Aurora live – by granting her treatment in the animal hospital. It was also Guillermo who designed this advanced brainwave scanning machine for people to enter the computer world without headsets – which Aurora made use of.

Evelyn looked at the time and realised it was already past

midnight. A large-scale mountain search operation was coming up at dawn, and right now, Guillermo would either be sound asleep or doing some last-minute preparations.

Impatient though she was, Evelyn knew she had to keep the good news to herself – at least for now.

CHAPTER 17

Victor's Robot Lair

Evelyn made sure she was fully charged that night. She took a short nap and, at daybreak, went down to the school gate with her friends. Groups of students had already gathered there for the mountain search operation. Some locals from nearby villages had also come to join the hunt for Victor's robots.

"How many robots do you think we're going to catch today?" Momoko asked, her voice brimming with enthusiasm.

"Anything from one to a hundred is possible," Heewon replied sagely. "It all comes down to whether our enemy gets wind of what we're about to do!"

An event tent had been erected on the lawn. Master Lin was standing inside, keeping watch on crates of weapons. Other teachers were weaving in and out of the gathered crowd, putting students into groups of eight to ten – electric guns were distributed to all team members, while the team leaders were each given an extra flame gun and three hand grenades.

The whole school set off together. They hiked up a mountain path near their school. It was a path everyone had walked many times, but today, students saw shadows everywhere they went – every movement seemed suspicious.

Around Evelyn, people frequently drew out their weapons, ready to shoot … only to find that they were pointing at some scampering squirrels, frightened birds or squealing monkeys.

They found nothing in the first fifteen minutes.

Master Khan, who was supervising the mountain search operation, suddenly shouted at a large group of students walking near him: "Spread out, everyone! Look under bushes, go into caves, search all the hidden places. Seriously, you can't expect to find a single robot when a hundred of us are marching up the hill with weapons!"

This new strategy worked.

Barely five minutes later, a group of students were yelling with excitement. Evelyn saw sparks in the air as electric shots were fired at a robot. The robot put up quite a struggle: he not only dodged all the electric shots, but also counter-attacked by breathing fire at everyone around him.

Students jumped back in panic. The team leader was quick-witted though: he bravely stood his ground and fired his flame gun at the robot with deadly precision.

The fire-breathing robot was instantly turned into a fireball. Evelyn winced as she prepared to hear the robot's screams … which never came. The robot did try to extinguish the fire – by frantically rolling himself on the ground – to no avail.

It took some time for the fire to die down. The leader of Evelyn's team then decided they should jog up and have a closer look: the robot's human skin had been completely burnt away, and all that was left of him was an exposed, badly damaged metal core.

For a moment, Evelyn was very aware that she too had a metal core. *But I'm different,* she reminded herself. *Victor's robots are here to wreak destruction. I'm here to bring peace.*

Ahead of them, mountain peaks loomed up. Evelyn looked back and spotted Guillermo coming up with three other teachers. Guillermo caught her eyes, waved, and quickened his pace towards her.

"You're going on a special mission with me," he told her in a mysterious voice.

"What are we going to do?" Evelyn asked, intrigued.

"Get your flying armour ready – we're flying up to Victor's robot lair!"

"To do what?" Evelyn exclaimed, shocked. *Didn't Master Chow say we are just going to search the mountains and destroy any Victor's robot we see?*

"To destroy the lair, obviously," said Guillermo, looking very determined.

Evelyn felt a chill run down her spine but put on a brave face.

"I'm ready. Let's go!" she bellowed.

Despite the danger they were about to face, flying in the sky side by side with Guillermo brought back all kinds of happy memories. It also reminded Evelyn of Aurora. Evelyn told Guillermo all about Aurora's special power in the computer world – how she entered through the brainwave scanning machine … grew big and majestic … becoming almost like the sacred eagle they saw in that roofless Buddhist temple.

Guillermo listened intently. He was surprised, as this was unexpected.

"Well done, Evelyn," he congratulated her. "I'm glad you find something that resonates with your heart and enhances your fighting power in the computer world."

The way Guillermo described Aurora sounded very familiar to Evelyn.

"Does that mean Aurora's my personal weapon?" she asked suddenly.

"I'm sure you don't want anyone calling your special bird a weapon –"

"No, of course not," Evelyn said quickly.

"But still, I dare say you'll find a powerful bird like her extremely useful in the computer world, especially in the fight against Victor." He smiled at her.

They landed in some bushes next to Victor's lair.

Guillermo spoke into his headset, "Chow, we are at the safe spot. All calm. Awaiting your signal to proceed."

Master Chow, who had been monitoring the whole mountain search operation from the war rooms, answered instantly, "Excellent. Everything's looking fine on my screens too. Let me just release the drones carrying our extra-strength EMP bombs from base, and then you are good to go."

Wow, electromagnetic pulse bombs! thought Evelyn, impressed. *I didn't know we are going to use those.*

"Three, two, one – firing!" Chow shouted.

Evelyn watched as ten drones, each carrying an EMP bomb, travelled speedily across the sky and headed straight to the front entrance of Victor's robot lair. Fire and explosions broke out in the sky as most of the drones were immediately shot down by automatic defence systems and robot guards at the cave mouth.

Two EMP bombs got in though, which were more than enough. If all went according to plan, the EMP bombs would wreak havoc to all electronic equipment inside: Victor's robots, computers, machines, defences, booby traps …

"Bingo!" Master Chow's excited voice came through Guillermo's headset.

"Follow me!" Guillermo said to Evelyn, leading the way into Victor's lair to finish off any remaining robots.

The robot guards at the entrance had all been disabled by the EMP bombs – they had slumped to the ground, their limbs bent at awkward angles. Inside the cave, there was a power blackout. Evelyn and Guillermo both activated their night visions. They scanned for hidden explosives every few steps and detonated them before moving forward. A boulder suddenly slid down from the side, triggering a series of loud and powerful explosions. Evelyn and Guillermo jumped back just in time.

They moved deeper into the large, multi-level robot lair. Looking around, Evelyn found herself in a Victor's factory, surrounded by shelves of heads, buckets of eyeballs, trays of fingernails …

A wave of nausea passed over Evelyn. She clenched her teeth and swallowed hard. But the nightmare didn't end there. She could now see plenty of headless robots suspended upside down from a conveyor belt – some of these bodies were completely metal, others looked very human.

Evelyn turned away in disgust.

There was an acrid smell of burning lingering in the air. White smoke was billowing from some of the machines inside the cave.

"Short circuits caused by the EMP bombs," Guillermo muttered.

The elevators were disabled too. However, since their scanner picked up movement in the lower levels, they decided to fly down to investigate.

"Get your electric gun ready," said Guillermo. He held out his flame gun, and together, they flew down a few levels in search of the source of movement.

Towards the back of the cave, they could see lights flickering. The electronics there appeared to be intact. The movement signal from Guillermo's scanner was growing stronger and stronger. Guillermo dashed forward, leading the way. Any moment now, they could be facing a swarm of hostile robots!

Blip – the movement signal weakened from five bars to half a bar all of a sudden. Guillermo slowed down and shook the scanner in frustration.

"We've lost them," he told Evelyn.

"Chow, do you have eyes on the escaped robots?" He spoke into the headset tensely.

Master Chow's voice came back loud and clear: "Keep chasing! Victor's robots are heading downhill. Go a hundred and twenty metres to your right. That's your nearest exit."

Guillermo brightened up.

"Let's go," he shouted, taking Evelyn's hand.

They dashed through the deserted cave and came out into the open. Evelyn caught a glimpse of the evil robots running downhill towards the forest – there were so many of them. Yet one was towering over the others and was clearly their leader. He wore a shiny metal armour, had a giant muscular body, and in his right arm was … a cannon!

Evelyn shivered. A strange idea struck her: *Can that be Victor in a real-world body?* She strained her eyes and focused, but before she could get a clear enough image, the entire group had moved into the dense forest.

Guillermo yelled into his headset, "Chow, where have the robots gone?"

They could hear non-stop typing sounds as Master Chow

tried to get Victor's robots back on his radar.

"Got them!" Chow exclaimed confidently. "They are near the nature reserve." Next second, his tone took a dramatic turn. He cried out in alarm, "Good Lord! They are attacking our students."

Guillermo frowned. He checked the coordinates Master Chow sent him and flew there immediately with Evelyn.

While in the sky, Evelyn was shocked to hear Chow confirm her worst fears –

"Listen, both of you, I've just found out Victor had taken up a real-world body. Watch out for that giant robot with a cannon!"

They landed at the nature reserve, where complete mayhem had broken out. There were even more evil robots than Evelyn expected. Some enclosures had been bombed, and animals were roaming freely. Students, armed with electric guns, were trying to hold off the charging robots valiantly. But there were too many enemies – some teams were swarmed, others were ambushed.

Evelyn suddenly sensed sneaky movements on a tree behind her. Next moment, an evil robot had landed on her back. He had both hands around her neck and was strangling her with a vice-like grip.

Evelyn immediately fired electric shots from her flying armour to get the robot off her back. She turned and found her attacker lying sprawled on the ground, utterly motionless.

Next second, Evelyn heard loud and heavy footsteps coming in her direction – four robots with machine guns were charging at her.

Evelyn wasn't intimidated; she was enraged and in full battle mode. Narrowing her eyes like a lioness, she swiftly identified the weak spots in each of the robots, then leapt out and kicked them fast and hard!

Two of the robots slumped to the ground right away, but the other two managed to flee despite being kicked. Evelyn chased after them. One of them turned around and tried to aim his machine gun at Evelyn, but Evelyn had started jumping and crouching.

As she crouched, Evelyn retrieved a sword lodged into the motionless body of a fallen robot. She used it to jab at her two enemies repeatedly. The two evil robots lost power and collapsed onto the ground one after another, broken.

Evelyn took their machine guns, feeling triumphant. But her good feeling was short-lived. Looking around, she realised other students weren't as successful in their fight against Victor's robots as she was.

The team leaders were dashing around with their flame guns trying to make sure everyone was accounted for. This was easier said than done as Victor's robots were breathing fire and throwing powerful explosives everywhere. To avoid catching fire or being killed by flying shrapnel, students were running all over the hillside, becoming easy targets once they were separated from their team.

On Evelyn's left, an injured student lay gasping on the ground. He looked up helplessly as an evil robot loomed over him. The robot reached down and grabbed him by his neck, lifting him mercilessly.

"I'm going to cut off your arms, one by one, till you bleed to death," the robot said with a devilish smile.

The student stared back, a look of determination on his face.

He screamed when the robot dug a sword into his left arm.

The sword didn't go deep, because at that moment Evelyn fired a bullet straight to the robot's on-off switch – disabling the robot immediately, and saving the student his arm.

Evelyn quickly moved on – she needed to save as many students as possible. Their side was losing, and with every passing second, someone could be losing an arm, a leg or even her life.

Victor, I'm going to kill you! thought Evelyn, who was feeling so angry that she wanted to fire a rocket right at Victor's face and rip him into a thousand pieces! The problem was: *Where's the devil?* Evelyn did a 360-degree scan but it revealed nothing. She cursed under her breath.

On Evelyn's right, a girl – bruised and bleeding – staggered amid the trees. A group of robots approached and she crouched behind a tree, hoping they wouldn't see her.

Evelyn hid behind another tree. She focused on the robots, waiting for the right moment to strike them …

"Something's coming!" one of the robots shouted all of a sudden, looking alarmed.

Guillermo, who had been running up and down the hill to rescue his students, was back by Evelyn's side. Evelyn could hear Master Chow shouting tensely, "Look out! There's a tsunami of heat signatures heading your way – so many – they are overlapping each other –"

Evelyn widened her eyes in sudden realisation.

"The animals are coming," she bellowed. The feeling was so strong it radiated from her heart and tingled all over her body.

The ground began to shake. Dozens of charging pandas, led by

Lola, crashed out of the bamboo forest.

"What the –" Guillermo exclaimed in shock.

Victor's robots tried to run, but they were crushed in the stampede, their metal parts scattering all over the ground.

Nearby, a group of Victor's robots turned their heads – fear and surprise on their faces – as Tyson jumped out of the bushes behind them. The evil robots were savaged by the fox-leopard. They fired frantically as they went down, hitting each other in a frenzy.

Evelyn watched in awe as screeching monkeys, Hank the golden monkey among them, bounced out of the bushes and chased after the surviving robots. Panicked yelling of the robots filled the air as they desperately ran for their lives.

Victor has enraged the animals of the nature reserve. This is payback time! thought Evelyn, relishing this moment of revenge.

"Let's find Victor and finish him off," said Guillermo, taking her hand.

They flew into the sky together, rising above the raging fire and thick smoke. It was difficult to see through the smoke, but after a while, they spotted him: the towering, cannon-wielding Victor. His mighty army was gone, and there were just a few robots running after him.

Evelyn felt an immediate boost in spirit.

"Check this out!" said Guillermo.

He had sent her a map, which showed a trap. Master Chow had located a dead-end cave in the middle of the hill, and their task was to bring Victor into it.

Below them, Victor looked up and realised he was being followed. Unfortunately for him, this part of the hill was mostly grassland with hardly any cover. He hurried up and soon came upon the cave Master Chow identified, which appeared to be the only hiding place in sight.

Victor paused in front of the cave entrance. After a second's hesitation, he bent his tall body and dashed headlong into it.

The students who happened to be around the cave jumped into action – they gave chase to Victor. Guillermo flew down from the sky to stop them.

"I'll handle the inside. Keep watch at the perimeter!" he ordered.

Evelyn followed Guillermo into the cave – it was wide and meandering. They glided through the tunnel in their flying gear and soon spotted Victor. He was running as fast as he could, desperate to get out from another exit before being caught up.

All of a sudden, Victor stopped. He had reached the end of the tunnel – a dead end.

What Victor did next was beyond Evelyn's wildest imagination. Instead of turning back and going on a killing rampage, Victor detonated himself and disappeared into a puff of purple gas. As the smoke cleared up, all that remained of Victor was his real-world body, giant in size and badly burnt, lying lifelessly on the cave floor.

"Where's he gone?" Guillermo shouted into his headset gruffly.

Master Chow's blood-chilling answer echoed through the dead-end cave tunnel: "Come back now. Victor has abandoned his real-world body and returned to the computer world."

A large group of students had gathered outside the cave, ready to help. They rushed up when they saw Guillermo and Evelyn. Guillermo frankly broke the news to them.

"You mean that robot with a cannon was Victor in a real

body?" a girl screamed in disbelief.

"How could he vanish into thin air?" another girl yelled indignantly.

"And after all this fighting, he was back in the computer world, safe and sound?" a male voice added with fury.

The cave soon erupted into chaotic shouting as everyone vented their frustration together.

Guillermo clapped his hands to call for order.

"Listen, boys and girls, we're done here. If you're still in the fight, come with me now to the VR computer lab."

The news that Victor had escaped into the computer world spread quickly. While local villagers and teachers stayed behind to keep watch on the captured robots, students raced to the VR computer lab, ready to continue the fight in the computer world.

The time had come to put their training to the test.

CHAPTER 18

The Prince and his Palace

Evelyn came out in the middle of the sea alongside Guillermo. It was sunset in the computer world. Looking over her shoulder, she could see more than a hundred students popping out of the sea within seconds. Each of them was dressed in a bullet-proof combat suit and carrying a camouflage backpack bulging with weapons.

Guillermo blew a whistle and gestured everyone to swim forward.

Once on shore, they had to climb up a cliff. Evelyn had just reached the top when she heard two loud bangs. A girl standing next to her began muttering repeatedly, "Oh my God!"

Evelyn looked down and saw two lifeless bodies lying on the rocky shore, their combat suits soaked with blood. It was nightmarish. She had never seen anything like that.

Then, something bizarre happened. The bodies blinked a few times and simply disappeared: one moment they were there, the other they were not! The two students had been sent back to the VR computer lab – it was game over for them.

Afterwards, everyone grew more cautious. Guillermo raised his sword – it was no ordinary sword, but a sword pulsing with electricity. Evelyn quickly unsheathed her Chinese long sword to get ready. They could now see Victor's palace in front of them. It seemed quite peaceful at the moment. *But who knows?* thought Evelyn.

A muscular student volunteered to set up the climbing ropes. He dashed forward and threw the ropes over the palace wall with his strong arms. He then tried to anchor the ropes. But as soon as his fingers touched the wall … ZAP! Part of the wall lighted up as if an electric current had just run through it.

The burly student was thrown back with great force, landing a few metres away. He stood up quickly and walked back to the palace wall, eager to try again.

"Wait!" someone shouted. "Why not check the sides and back. There's got to be another way in."

"We should look for openings, holes, even gaps," another voice chimed in.

While students were discussing how best to get into Victor's palace, Master Chow's voice could be heard coming from Guillermo's gear. Everyone immediately quieted down to listen.

"Ronald suggested launching missiles to the palace wall to blast a hole. What do you think?" said Master Chow to Guillermo.

Around Evelyn, students' eyes lit up in wonder.

"Good idea, let's proceed!" Guillermo replied in a cool and sensible tone.

They all looked up with anticipation. Presently, three missiles rocketed into the sky and sped towards the palace. They were launched from a missile silo that had just sprung up over the horizon – Evelyn was sure the facility wasn't there a minute ago.

The missiles were a spectacular sight. Some students started clapping, but stopped when they saw the palace's defence system launching its own missiles to intercept the intruding ones. The missiles from both sides met in the sky and exploded deafeningly above their heads, shaking the palace and the land beyond.

Students screamed and ran for cover as burning shrapnel showered back to the ground.

The missiles clearly didn't work, but Guillermo had some good news: Ronald had just found a shortcut into Victor's palace.

There was a catch.

"It will require diving into the lake," Guillermo warned his students, "which is far more difficult than swimming."

"No worries. We'll manage!" a thrilled voice cried out. Lots of students whooped and cheered in agreement.

"We will come out from a pond inside the palace," Guillermo continued, his expression grave. "We don't know yet what lies outside that pond."

There were whispers of voices as students spoke of the monsters and horrors that could be awaiting them on the other side …

In the end, it was decided that a team of twenty would go first. Guillermo took Evelyn's hand and urged her to follow him.

"Any tips on how to survive the dive?" asked Evelyn, looking into the bottomless lake uncertainly.

"The key is to focus," Guillermo gazed at her, his blue eyes glittering with purpose. "Remember the Knight Alley? Same principle here. Just concentrate on the exit and swim as fast as you can towards it."

Evelyn broke into a little smile. *All right, this is just another version of the Knight Alley.*

Guillermo patted her shoulder encouragingly: "Let's go!"

Evelyn took several deep breaths, then plunged into the lake.

It was a very long dive. She swam on and on, and wondered how far she was from the exit. Evelyn felt suffocated. She thought she was going to drown. Then all of a sudden, she saw light in front of her.

Evelyn redoubled her efforts, but the end was further than it appeared. When she finally came out of the pond inside Victor's palace, Evelyn gasped for air: *Phew, that was close!*

She looked around. There were exactly fourteen people around her. They were in a huge, circular chamber. Guillermo frowned and confirmed that five students didn't make it.

They jumped out of the pond together. No sooner had they left the pond than cracking noises sounded above their heads. Evelyn's first thought was that the dome-shaped ceiling, which arched high above them and was covered with paintings of fire-breathing dragons, was about to collapse.

She was wrong.

She looked up and saw a hole had opened up in the ceiling. Three actual dragons had just got in: they had evil red eyes, tough scales that covered their bodies like armours, and thick tails that were full of razor-sharp spikes. Evelyn and her teammates jumped out of the way hastily as one of the dragons blew a jet of flame in their direction.

"How in the computer world do we slay these dragons?" asked a female student in a shaky voice.

"We don't kill the dragons," Guillermo answered, "we distract them."

Zoom! The three dragons suddenly left the ceiling and swooped down swiftly to a door at the side of the chamber. They flied around the door, eyeing Evelyn and her teammates with hostility, but didn't cross over to attack them.

"To reach Victor's private chamber, we have to go through that door," said Guillermo, glancing at the three dragons warily. "Evelyn and I will go first, to plant some bombs. We need your help in distracting the dragons –"

"Trust us, we're more than capable!" a heavily built male student answered zealously, swinging a hammer in one hand and an axe in another.

Guillermo nodded to show his approval.

"Once we've planted the bombs, I'll give you a signal to storm in and finish off Victor."

Everyone quickly moved into position. And while their team distracted the dragons with calls and weapons, Evelyn and Guillermo dashed across the chamber and slipped past the previously guarded door.

There was another door, which creaked open forbiddingly. Guillermo showed Evelyn some explosives hidden inside his combat suit. He then sneaked to the side and disappeared.

Evelyn walked in.

Victor's private chamber was grand and extravagant. The walls and ceiling were covered with gold. The chandelier was made of pieces of large diamonds. Countless rubies, sapphires and emeralds adorned the place, reflecting the light dazzlingly.

At first, Evelyn saw no one.

Then the royal chair in the centre of the chamber turned. Victor was seated on the throne. His princely figure was a far cry from that giant robot body Evelyn last saw him in. Right now, Victor was staring at Evelyn with such cold, merciless eyes she immediately felt a shiver down her spine.

"How does it feel to betray your own kind?" he asked in an obnoxiously silky voice.

Evelyn was unnerved for a moment, but regained her composure fast enough.

"It doesn't matter what 'kind' I am. I am on the righteous side, and that's all you need to know," she told him straight to his face. Glancing around secretively, Evelyn wondered: *Now, where's Guillermo planting the bombs?*

"I see you really believe you are human," said Victor mockingly. "How terribly misguided you are!"

"You're the one who's misguided, not me," Evelyn retorted bravely. "I'm not like you, Victor. I don't kill innocent people for fun."

As she spoke, something caught Evelyn's eyes: a helicopter! It blended into the background so flawlessly she almost missed it – golden, sparkling, and adorned with precious stones, the helicopter looked just like everything else in Victor's private chamber.

Evelyn could vaguely see Guillermo's feet under the helicopter. He was tying explosives to it. She looked away hurriedly to avoid drawing Victor's attention to the helicopter.

Luckily, Victor was focusing his cold black eyes entirely on Evelyn.

"You're an idiot, Evelyn Smith," he sighed, his tone extremely arrogant, "fraternising with the enemy, and not knowing all the great things our kind can achieve together …"

At that moment, the helicopter exploded. Metal shards flew in all directions. The whole palace shook, and the diamond chandelier came crashing down from the ceiling thunderously.

Amid the smoke and dust, Evelyn saw Victor jump up from his throne, enraged and seething with fury.

"You and your pathetic friends are all going to die tonight!"

he growled.

"No one's going to die tonight," Evelyn shouted at Victor fearlessly, "except you!"

Victor unsheathed a medieval sword from his belt and lunged at Evelyn.

Guillermo leapt out from behind a pillar to block him. As Guillermo's sword collided with Victor's, a sharp clink echoed through the debris-filled chamber. Evelyn could see blue electric pulses from Guillermo's sword pushing their way towards Victor's sword.

Victor broke away just before the electric pulses reached his hand.

Evelyn, armed with her Chinese long sword, seized the chance to pounce on Victor, slashing at him with her sword.

Victor jumped back agilely and let out a demonic, high-pitched laugh.

The side doors of the chamber suddenly burst open: throwing knives and flaming arrows came flying in Victor's direction. Evelyn was amazed to see her teammates barge in. They ran towards Victor, yelling fiercely as they closed in on him.

"That's Victor!"

"Kill him!"

"Don't let him get away!"

Victor blocked and parried the weapons thrown at him with the flat of his sword. He jumped around and jabbed at the students with all his might. But still, within seconds, his princely gown was in tatters and splattered with his own blood – several places on his arms were cut by the flying blades, his left eyebrow was singed by a flaming arrow that dropped from above, and he almost got trapped in a net thrown at him.

Injured and in pain, Victor the prince uttered a deep guttural roar: he started spinning rapidly on the spot. There was a blur as dust and rubbles swirled up around him.

Evelyn blinked and then saw, to her disbelief, that Victor had mutated into a vampire. He spread out his vampire cloak like wings and flew out of an open window.

Evelyn and Guillermo immediately dashed towards the window. They were closely followed by their team. Students were shouting tensely: "Don't let him go!"

Evelyn looked down from the window: she could see a bat-like figure sprinting across the courtyard and quickly disappearing under some trees. The window was several storeys from the ground.

"We've got to find some climbing ropes!" one of the students suggested in a loud voice.

The others agreed. They turned back and began to search Victor's palace for tools.

Evelyn and Guillermo lingered at the window for a bit longer. Guillermo was speaking to Master Chow, seeking his advice – so far, climbing ropes remained the best option.

Evelyn was about to turn back when from the corner of her eye, she caught sight of a giant, gorgeous bird fast approaching – Aurora had entered the computer world. The magnificent bird glided effortlessly across the night sky. She came straight to Evelyn, hovering right outside the window of Victor's private chamber, her face expectant.

Evelyn eagerly stepped out onto the window ledge and climbed onto Aurora's back. She looked back to wave goodbye to Guillermo.

Guillermo held her hand tightly.

"Be careful, Evelyn – I'll catch up with you in a moment."

Then he let go of her hand and the giant bird took Evelyn into the night sky.

Aurora circled the sky in search of Victor. Once she spotted him, whoosh, she dived down purposefully. Evelyn and Aurora crashed through leaves and branches, landing in the courtyard.

Six palace guards darted towards them – the guards pointed their rifles at Evelyn and Aurora. Victor was a dark figure under a tree. The silver blade of his medieval sword glinted ominously in the yellowish palace light.

"Back off!" he barked at the guards.

"You really think you can beat me, don't you?" he growled at Evelyn contemptuously, his red vampire eyes shimmering with pure evil.

Victor the vampire then lunged at Evelyn with lightning speed, driving his sword at her chest with one powerful thrust – he meant to kill.

Evelyn leapt aside, but Victor still managed to slash at her shoulder. She yelled in pain as blood poured out of her wound.

Evelyn roared, determined to defeat Victor.

Victor's speed was supernatural, and Evelyn suffered several more slashes to her body before she got used to his lightning speed. She was focused, fearless, determined to fight Victor till her last breath.

Clinks and clanks rang out through the courtyard as their two swords struck each other over and over again. The fight was set to drag on. Evelyn didn't know how much longer she could persevere. Then, all of a sudden, Aurora joined the fight. The magnificent bird flew into Victor's face, temporarily blinding him with her huge wings.

Evelyn seized the opportunity to thrust her sword into

Victor's heart.

Victor exclaimed in shock and entered into a rapid spin immediately. When the spinning stopped, there was no prince, no vampire, not even a dead body left. Victor had turned into a plume of white smoke. A breeze swept across the courtyard, carrying the white smoke into the restless night …

Evelyn sighed heavily and collapsed to the ground. She closed her eyes and let her body go limp.

Aurora cried out in a shrill voice, as if signalling for help.

Evelyn felt the ground tremble. Next second, she felt Guillermo by her side, talking to her, holding her hands …

Then, she lost consciousness completely.

CHAPTER 19

A Well-Deserved Break

Evelyn woke up feeling disorientated. She was sitting on a sofa facing the window. The room was quite dark, and outside, the sky was blue and gold.

Evelyn could vaguely hear Guillermo and Master Chow talking in the room next door. She sniffed, and an invigorating smell of chocolate cakes immediately filled her nostrils.

Suddenly, Evelyn felt fully alive.

"Yes!" she yelled in delight. Evelyn jumped out of the sofa, saw the oven glowing in the darkness, and quickly dashed towards it to check whether the cakes were ready.

She had just knelt down in front of the oven when the door opened and the lights were switched on. Master Chow and Guillermo walked in.

"Good morning, Evelyn, nice to see you up and about!" Master Chow greeted her warmly, grinning.

Evelyn felt awkward. It struck her that she was in the living room of Headmaster Mansion, caught trying to steal cakes from the oven.

"Hi," she mumbled and quickly got back to the sofa.

Master Chow sat down next to her.

"It feels good to be back in the real world, isn't it?" he said kindly.

That reminded Evelyn. "Did I die in the computer world?" she blurted.

"No, Evelyn, you did not," Master Chow replied. "You fainted though, so Guillermo pressed your button to bring you back."

"Where's Victor now?" asked Evelyn, growing anxious. "Where did he go after turning into white smoke?"

"Hopefully, he's gone for good, but we're not sure," said Chow, frowning slightly. "Ronald and his team of scientists are still examining the computer data."

Guillermo came out of the kitchen carrying a large tray laden with chocolate brownies, iced doughnuts and fruit tarts.

"The point is," he interjected brightly, "Victor's gone for now. The world gets to enjoy a break, and you, Evelyn, certainly deserve some desserts!"

Master Chow quickly stood up to make room for Guillermo.

"Well, I've got to go. You two – enjoy yourselves," he said with a smile.

Once Master Chow had left, Evelyn cosied up to Guillermo and ate all the desserts he made her – she was starving.

"How long have I been in here?" she asked, licking her lips.

"Overnight," Guillermo answered, gazing at her.

"Did you – er – fix me?" she added uncertainly.

"I did some checks on you. I feared you were injured. Luckily, you were just tired, so I let you rest."

"How's Aurora?" Evelyn asked suddenly.

"I went to look for her after bringing you here. She was in the IT Centre, hopping smugly next to the brainwave scanning machine …"

The doorbell buzzed. Guillermo went to open the front door. Evelyn heard voices from the corridor. Next moment, Heewon, Momoko, Lily and Xiaojin came bursting into the room.

"Evelyn!" they squealed with delight and dashed forward to hug her.

"We were so worried about you!" said Lily, wrapping her arms around Evelyn. "Last night, we saw the headmaster taking you on his hoverboard. You were not moving at all –"

"Evelyn, is it true that you defeated Victor in a sword fight?" Heewon asked, her brown eyes wide with admiration.

"Well, I managed to put a sword through his heart," said Evelyn, who couldn't help feeling pleased with herself.

"Thank goodness!" Xiaojin gasped.

"Mind you, it is still too early to say whether Victor is really dead ..." Evelyn added uneasily.

"You saved us, Evelyn!" said Heewon, leaning forward to give Evelyn a big hug. "That's what matters most."

Evelyn broke into a smile.

"So what about you? What happened while you kept watch outside Victor's palace?"

"You wouldn't believe what we saw!" Momoko cried out. Then, in a mysterious voice, she told Evelyn how they were swarmed by hyenas ("They had abnormally long fangs, clearly genetically modified by Victor to be venomous"), and shot by expert snipers ("There were loads of them, lucky we were all wearing our bullet-proof combat suits").

Evelyn listened tensely, outraged by the horrors Victor inflicted on her friends.

After that, they moved on to merrier topics: gossips, relationships, and their summer plans. While they talked, Xiaojin handed Evelyn her fruit basket.

"Try these," Xiaojin said enthusiastically, "freshly picked from the university's edible forest."

Evelyn vividly remembered what the edible forest looked like – it was full of crooked trees and wild weeds! Hesitantly, she tried a few lychees and figs from the fruit basket. To her amazement, they were quite delicious.

Guillermo came in shortly afterwards.

"Time's up. Evelyn needs to rest," he said, looking sternly at them.

"I'm not tired!" Evelyn protested, but her friends seemed to agree with Guillermo.

"Bye Evelyn –"

"Rest well!"

"See you later –"

"And don't forget the feast this evening, at the Great Hall."

"I won't," Evelyn promised.

Evelyn spent the rest of the day in sleep mode – she was alone as Guillermo had gone to Master Chow's office. When she woke up again, the sun was already setting.

Oh no! Evelyn jumped up in panic. *If I don't hurry up, I'm going to be late for the feast!*

She quickly pulled on her kung fu robe, tied her hair in a bun, and ran as fast as she could from Headmaster Mansion to the Great Hall.

When Evelyn arrived, the Great Hall was already full and the babble was quite loud. Students were chatting around the banquet tables, which were draped with red embroidered cloths. Evelyn saw Heewon and Lily waving at her. She smiled and strolled towards their table.

Someone must have spotted Evelyn … because all of a

sudden, people stopped talking. An awkward silence fell on the hall: everyone was staring at her!

Evelyn quickly slid into the seat her friends had reserved for her. To her relief, chatter filled the hall again as soon as she sat down.

Up on the stage where the teachers were seated, Master Chow and Guillermo got to their feet.

Master Lin struck the large bronze bell three times …

"Welcome to the end-of-semester feast," Master Chow said in his booming voice. "Before we begin, I would like to say a few words."

"First, a big thank you to every one of you – for standing up against Victor, defending the school, and fighting for a better world …"

Master Chow took off his academic cap to salute his students in a hearty manner. In response, students raised their glasses and cheered loudly.

"Second, I would like to applaud Evelyn Smith –"

All eyes were on Evelyn once more, and she felt her face and ears going scarlet.

"– for showing extraordinary courage, strength and determination in the fight against Victor."

The cheering and clapping that followed lasted for almost a minute. Evelyn stole a glance at Guillermo on the stage and found him beaming at her fondly.

"And so," Master Chow concluded cheerfully, "it's time for a break! You've earned it. Have a safe journey home and see you all after the summer vacation!"

The feast started right away. It was a sumptuous meal: they were served prawn crackers, Sichuan crispy ducks, dim sum platters, seafood rolls, suckling pigs with hoisin sauce, fried rice, chow mein, seasonal fruits …

After the meal, the banquet tables and chairs were cleared away to make way for a large glowing dance floor. Heewon and Momoko were eager to dance with the strong, beefy boys in their class, while Xiaojin and Lily were partial to the leaner, more agile types.

Evelyn shrugged and kept to herself. For her, life was complicated enough as it was.

The evening ended with a spectacular fireworks celebration out in the wild.

Over the next week, Evelyn's friends left campus one by one to catch their flights home. They were overjoyed and couldn't wait to see their families.

Evelyn, however, felt very differently. For one thing, she didn't have any family member she knew of; for another, she had to call a cold and oppressive robot factory her home. As the semester had ended two weeks early in the aftermath of Victor's attacks, Evelyn decided she would relax and stay till the original end date of the semester.

"It's up to you," said Guillermo. "I'll be here to oversee repair works on campus anyway."

Evelyn spent her days playing with Aurora and the animals in the nature reserve. Like Aurora, the animals were all back to their usual selves: the pandas were as cuddly and carefree as ever, the monkeys were naughty and noisy, and Tyson was once again that bloodthirsty beast he always was. It was hard to believe they could fight so well in the hour of need … but then, that was what happened.

Before long, it was time for Evelyn to head back to London.

That morning, Guillermo walked Evelyn to the airfield. Ronald had booked her a seat on a supersonic private jet. Evelyn looked around to see who she would be flying with: there were several men in black suits, a vet from the nature reserve, and a group of bleary-eyed tourists surrounded by piles of luggage.

After months of living on campus with her friends and schoolmates, the prospect of leaving China with these strangers overwhelmed Evelyn with loneliness. Worse still, she had to spend her summer vacation all alone in Ronald's factory. *How am I going to survive that?*

Unbidden tears pooled in Evelyn's eyes. Guillermo patted her shoulder gently.

"Evelyn, if you need anything, just give me a call –"

"But you're so far away!" Evelyn whined.

"I've got friends in London," Guillermo answered, gazing into Evelyn's eyes. "Just call me, all right?"

Evelyn nodded. The two of them hugged briefly.

"See you next semester," said Guillermo.

The supersonic jet took off at once, and by the time Evelyn had the mood to look out of the window, she was already 30 km up in the sky. All she could see was an infinitely deep and mysterious universe, which reflected the uncertainty Evelyn felt about going back to Ronald's factory … even if it was just for the summer.

ABOUT THE AUTHOR

Kwan Wu was born and raised in Hong Kong, a special administrative region of China. She holds a BA in English Studies from the University of Hong Kong. *Evelyn and the Kung Fu Headmaster* is her first novel.

Lightning Source UK Ltd.
Milton Keynes UK
UKHW012047070221
378383UK00001B/27